Wee Willie Winkie by Rudyard Kipling

Rudyard Kipling: A great Victorian, a great writer of Empire, a great man.

Rudyard Kipling was one of the most popular writers of prose and poetry in the late 19th and 20th Century and awarded the Noble Prize for Literature in 1907.

Born in Bombay on 30th December 1865, as was the custom in those days, he and his sister were sent back to England when he was 5. The ill-treatment and cruelty by the couple who they boarded with in Portsmouth, Kipling himself suggested, contributed to the onset of his literary life. This was further enhanced by his return to India at age 16 to work on a local paper, as not only did this result in him writing constantly but also made him explore issues of identity and national allegiance which pervade much of his work.

Whilst he is best remembered for his classic children's stories and his popular poem 'If...' he is also regarded as a major innovator in the art of the short story.

Index of Contents

Wee Willie Winkie
Baa Baa, Black Sheep
The First Bag
The Second Bag
The Third Bag
His Majesty the King
The Drums of the Fore and Aft
Rudyard Kipling – A Short Biography
Rudyard Kipling – A Concise Bibliography

I0684195

WEE WILLIE WINKIE

His full name was Percival William Williams, but he picked up the other name in a nursery-book, and that was the end of the christened titles. His mother's ayah called him Willie-Baba, but as he never paid the faintest attention to anything that the ayah said, her wisdom did not help matters.

His father was the Colonel of the 195th, and as soon as Wee Willie Winkie was old enough to understand what Military Discipline meant, Colonel Williams put him under it. There was no other way of managing the child. When he was good for a week, he drew good-conduct pay; and when he was bad, he was deprived of his good-conduct stripe. Generally he was bad, for India offers many chances of going wrong to little six-year-olds.

Children resent familiarity from strangers, and Wee Willie Winkie was a very particular child. Once he accepted an acquaintance, he was graciously pleased to thaw. He accepted Brandis, a subaltern of the 195th, on sight. Brandis was having tea at the Colonel's, and Wee Willie Winkie entered strong in the possession of a good-conduct badge won for not chasing the hens round the compound. He regarded Brandis with gravity for at least ten minutes, and then delivered himself of his opinion.

'I like you,' said he slowly, getting off his chair and coming over to Brandis. 'I like you. I shall call you Coppy, because of your hair. Do you mind being called Coppy? It is because of ve hair, you know.'

Here was one of the most embarrassing of Wee Willie Winkie's peculiarities. He would look at a stranger for some time, and then, without warning or explanation, would give him a name. And the name stuck. No regimental penalties could break Wee Willie Winkie of this habit. He lost his good-conduct badge for christening the Commissioner's wife 'Pobs'; but nothing that the Colonel could do made the Station forego the nickname, and Mrs. Collen remained 'Pobs' till the end of her stay. So Brandis was christened 'Coppy,' and rose, therefore, in the estimation of the regiment.

If Wee Willie Winkie took an interest in any one, the fortunate man was envied alike by the mess and the rank and file. And in their envy lay no suspicion of self-interest. 'The Colonel's son' was idolised on his own merits entirely. Yet Wee Willie Winkie was not lovely. His face was permanently freckled, as his legs were permanently scratched, and in spite of his mother's almost tearful remonstrances he had insisted upon having his long yellow locks cut short in the military fashion. 'I want my hair like Sergeant Tummil's,' said Wee Willie Winkie, and, his father abetting, the sacrifice was accomplished.

Three weeks after the bestowal of his youthful affections on Lieutenant Brandis—henceforward to be called 'Coppy' for the sake of brevity—Wee Willie Winkie was destined to behold strange things and far beyond his comprehension.

Coppy returned his liking with interest. Coppy had let him wear for five rapturous minutes his own big sword—just as tall as Wee Willie Winkie. Coppy had promised him a terrier puppy; and Coppy had permitted him to witness the miraculous operation of shaving. Nay, more—Coppy had said that even he, Wee Willie Winkie, would rise in time to the ownership of a box of shiny knives, a silver soap-box, and a silver-handled 'sputterbrush,' as Wee Willie Winkie called it. Decidedly, there was no one except his father, who could give or take away good-conduct badges at pleasure, half so wise, strong, and valiant as Coppy with the Afghan and Egyptian medals on his breast. Why, then, should Coppy be guilty of the unmanly weakness of kissing—vehemently kissing—a 'big girl,' Miss Allardyce to wit? In the course of a morning ride Wee Willie Winkie had seen Coppy so doing, and, like the gentleman he was, had promptly wheeled round and cantered back to his groom, lest the groom should also see.

Under ordinary circumstances he would have spoken to his father, but he felt instinctively that this was a matter on which Coppy ought first to be consulted.

'Coppy,' shouted Wee Willie Winkie, reining up outside that subaltern's bungalow early one morning—'I want to see you, Coppy!'

'Come in, young 'un,' returned Coppy, who was at early breakfast in the midst of his dogs. 'What mischief have you been getting into now?'

Wee Willie Winkie had done nothing notoriously bad for three days, and so stood on a pinnacle of virtue.

'I've been doing nothing bad,' said he, curling himself into a long chair with a studious affectation of the Colonel's languor after a hot parade. He buried his freckled nose in a tea-cup and, with eyes staring roundly over the rim, asked: 'I say, Coppy, is it pwoper to kiss big girls?'

'By Jove! You're beginning early. Who do you want to kiss?'

'No one. My muvver's always kissing me if I don't stop her. If it isn't pwoper, how was you kissing Major Allardyce's big girl last morning, by ve canal?'

Coppy's brow wrinkled. He and Miss Allardyce had with great craft managed to keep their engagement secret for a fortnight. There were urgent and imperative reasons why Major Allardyce should not know how matters stood for at least another month, and this small marplot had discovered a great deal too much.

'I saw you,' said Wee Willie Winkie calmly. 'But ve sais didn't see. I said, "Hut jao!" '

'Oh, you had that much sense, you young rip,' groaned poor Coppy, half amused and half angry. 'And how many people may you have told about it?'

'Only me myself. You didn't tell when I twied to wide ve buffalo ven my pony was lame; and I fought you wouldn't like.'

'Winkie,' said Coppy enthusiastically, shaking the small hand, 'you're the best of good fellows. Look here, you can't understand all these things. One of these days—hang it, how can I make you see it!—I'm going to marry Miss Allardyce, and then she'll be Mrs. Coppy, as you say. If your young mind is so scandalised at the idea of kissing big girls, go and tell your father.'

'What will happen?' said Wee Willie Winkie, who firmly believed that his father was omnipotent.

'I shall get into trouble,' said Coppy, playing his trump card with an appealing look at the holder of the ace.

'Ven I won't,' said Wee Willie Winkie briefly. 'But my faver says it's un-man-ly to be always kissing, and I didn't fink you'd do vat, Coppy.'

'I'm not always kissing, old chap. It's only now and then, and when you're bigger you'll do it too. Your father meant it's not good for little boys.'

'Ah!' said Wee Willie Winkie, now fully enlightened. 'It's like ve sputter-brush?'

'Exactly,' said Coppy gravely.

'But I don't fink I'll ever want to kiss big girls, nor no one, 'cept my muvver. And I must vat, you know.'

There was a long pause, broken by Wee Willie Winkie.

'Are you fond of vis big girl, Coppy?'

'Awfully!' said Coppy.

'Fonder van you are of Bell or ve Butcha—or me?'

'It's in a different way,' said Coppy. 'You see, one of these days Miss Allardyce will belong to me, but you'll grow up and command the Regiment and—all sorts of things. It's quite different, you see.'

'Very well,' said Wee Willie Winkie, rising. 'If you're fond of ve big girl I won't tell any one. I must go now.'

Coppy rose and escorted his small guest to the door, adding—'You're the best of little fellows, Winkie. I tell you what. In thirty days from now you can tell if you like—tell any one you like.'

Thus the secret of the Brandis-Allardyce engagement was dependent on a little child's word. Coppy, who knew Wee Willie Winkie's idea of truth, was at ease, for he felt that he would not break promises. Wee Willie Winkie betrayed a special and unusual interest in Miss Allardyce, and, slowly revolving round that embarrassed young lady, was used to regard her gravely with unwinking eye. He was trying to discover why Coppy should have kissed her. She was not half so nice as his own mother. On the other hand, she was Coppy's property, and would in time belong to him. Therefore it behoved him to treat her with as much respect as Coppy's big sword or shiny pistol.

The idea that he shared a great secret in common with Coppy kept Wee Willie Winkie unusually virtuous for three weeks. Then the Old Adam broke out, and he made what he called a 'camp-fire' at the bottom of the garden. How could he have foreseen that the flying sparks would have lighted the Colonel's little hay-rick and consumed a week's store for the horses? Sudden and swift was the punishment— deprivation of the good-conduct badge and, most sorrowful of all, two days' confinement to barracks— the house and verandah—coupled with the withdrawal of the light of his father's countenance.

He took the sentence like the man he strove to be, drew himself up with a quivering under-lip, saluted, and, once clear of the room, ran to weep bitterly in his nursery—called by him 'my quarters.' Coppy came in the afternoon and attempted to console the culprit.

'I'm under awwest,' said Wee Willie Winkie mournfully, 'and I didn't ought to speak to you.'

Very early the next morning he climbed on to the roof of the house—that was not forbidden—and beheld Miss Allardyce going for a ride.

'Where are you going?' cried Wee Willie Winkie.

'Across the river,' she answered, and trotted forward.

Now the cantonment in which the 195th lay was bounded on the north by a river—dry in the winter. From his earliest years, Wee Willie Winkie had been forbidden to go across the river, and had noted that even Coppy—the almost almighty Coppy—had never set foot beyond it. Wee Willie Winkie had once been read to, out of a big blue book, the history of the Princess and the Goblins—a most wonderful tale of a land where the Goblins were always warring with the children of men until they were defeated by one Curdie. Ever since that date it seemed to him that the bare black and purple hills across the river were inhabited by Goblins, and, in truth, every one had said that there lived the Bad Men. Even in his own house the lower halves of the windows were covered with green paper on account of the Bad Men who might, if allowed clear view, fire into peaceful drawing-rooms and comfortable bedrooms. Certainly, beyond the river, which was the end of all the Earth, lived the Bad Men. And here was Major Allardyce's big girl, Coppy's property, preparing to venture into their borders! What would Coppy say if anything happened to her? If the Goblins ran off with her as they did with Curdie's Princess? She must at all hazards be turned back.

The house was still. Wee Willie Winkie reflected for a moment on the very terrible wrath of his father; and then—broke his arrest! It was a crime unspeakable. The low sun threw his shadow, very large and very black, on the trim garden-paths, as he went down to the stables and ordered his pony. It seemed to him in the hush of the dawn that all the big world had been bidden to stand still and look at Wee Willie Winkie guilty of mutiny. The drowsy sais gave him his mount, and, since the one great sin made all others insignificant, Wee Willie Winkie said that he was going to ride over to Coppy Sahib, and went out at a foot-pace, stepping on the soft mould of the flower-borders.

The devastating track of the pony's feet was the last misdeed that cut him off from all sympathy of Humanity. He turned into the road, leaned forward, and rode as fast as the pony could put foot to the ground in the direction of the river.

But the liveliest of twelve-two ponies can do little against the long canter of a Waler. Miss Allardyce was far ahead, had passed through the crops, beyond the Police-posts, when all the guards were asleep, and her mount was scattering the pebbles of the river-bed as Wee Willie Winkie left the cantonment and British India behind him. Bowed forward and still flogging, Wee Willie Winkie shot into Afghan territory, and could just see Miss Allardyce, a black speck, flickering across the stony plain. The reason of her wandering was simple enough. Coppy, in a tone of too-hastily-assumed authority, had told her overnight that she must not ride out by the river. And she had gone to prove her own spirit and teach Coppy a lesson.

Almost at the foot of the inhospitable hills, Wee Willie Winkie saw the Waler blunder and come down heavily. Miss Allardyce struggled clear, but her ankle had been severely twisted, and she could not stand. Having fully shown her spirit, she wept, and was surprised by the apparition of a white, wide-eyed child in khaki, on a nearly spent pony.

'Are you badly, badly hurted?' shouted Wee Willie Winkie, as soon as he was within range. 'You didn't ought to be here.'

'I don't know,' said Miss Allardyce ruefully, ignoring the reproof. 'Good gracious, child, what are you doing here?'

'You said you was going acwoss ve wiver,' panted Wee Willie Winkie, throwing himself off his pony. 'And nobody—not even Coppy—must go acwoss ve wiver, and I came after you ever so hard, but you wouldn't stop, and now you've hurted yourself, and Coppy will be angwy wiv me, and—I've bwoken my awwest! I've bwoken my awwest!'

The future Colonel of the 195th sat down and sobbed. In spite of the pain in her ankle the girl was moved.

'Have you ridden all the way from cantonments, little man? What for?'

'You belonged to Coppy. Coppy told me so!' wailed Wee Willie Winkie disconsolately. 'I saw him kissing you, and he said he was fonder of you van Bell or ve Butcha or me. And so I came. You must get up and come back. You didn't ought to be here. Vis is a bad place, and I've bwoken my awwest.'

'I can't move, Winkie,' said Miss Allardyce, with a groan. 'I've hurt my foot. What shall I do?'

She showed a readiness to weep anew, which steadied Wee Willie Winkie, who had been brought up to believe that tears were the depth of unmanliness. Still, when one is as great a sinner as Wee Willie Winkie, even a man may be permitted to break down.

'Winkie,' said Miss Allardyce, 'when you've rested a little, ride back and tell them to send out something to carry me back in. It hurts fearfully.'

The child sat still for a little time and Miss Allardyce closed her eyes; the pain was nearly making her faint. She was roused by Wee Willie Winkie tying up the reins on his pony's neck and setting it free with a vicious cut of his whip that made it whicker. The little animal headed towards the cantonments.

'Oh, Winkie, what are you doing?'

'Hush!' said Wee Willie Winkie. 'Vere's a man coming—one of ve Bad Men. I must stay wiv you. My faver says a man must always look after a girl. Jack will go home, and ven vey'll come and look for us. Vat's why I let him go.'

Not one man but two or three had appeared from behind the rocks of the hills, and the heart of Wee Willie Winkie sank within him, for just in this manner were the Goblins wont to steal out and vex Curdie's soul. Thus had they played in Curdie's garden—he had seen the picture—and thus had they frightened the Princess's nurse. He heard them talking to each other, and recognised with joy the bastard Pushto that he had picked up from one of his father's grooms lately dismissed. People who spoke that tongue could not be the Bad Men. They were only natives after all.

They came up to the boulders on which Miss Allardyce's horse had blundered.

Then rose from the rock Wee Willie Winkie, child of the Dominant Race, aged six and three-quarters, and said briefly and emphatically 'Jao!' The pony had crossed the river-bed.

The men laughed, and laughter from natives was the one thing Wee Willie Winkie could not tolerate. He asked them what they wanted and why they did not depart. Other men with most evil faces and crooked-stocked guns crept out of the shadows of the hills, till, soon, Wee Willie Winkie was face to face with an audience some twenty strong. Miss Allardyce screamed.

'Who are you?' said one of the men.

'I am the Colonel Sahib's son, and my order is that you go at once. You black men are frightening the Miss Sahib. One of you must run into cantonments and take the news that the Miss Sahib has hurt herself, and that the Colonel's son is here with her.'

'Put our feet into the trap?' was the laughing reply. 'Hear this boy's speech!'

'Say that I sent you—I, the Colonel's son. They will give you money.'

'What is the use of this talk? Take up the child and the girl, and we can at least ask for the ransom. Ours are the villages on the heights,' said a voice in the background.

These were the Bad Men—worse than Goblins—and it needed all Wee Willie Winkie's training to prevent him from bursting into tears. But he felt that to cry before a native, excepting only his mother's ayah, would be an infamy greater than any mutiny. Moreover, he, as future Colonel of the 195th, had that grim regiment at his back.

'Are you going to carry us away?' said Wee Willie Winkie, very blanched and uncomfortable.

'Yes, my little Sahib Bahadur,' said the tallest of the men, 'and eat you afterwards.'

'That is child's talk,' said Wee Willie Winkie. 'Men do not eat men.'

A yell of laughter interrupted him, but he went on firmly—'And if you do carry us away, I tell you that all my regiment will come up in a day and kill you all without leaving one. Who will take my message to the Colonel Sahib?'

Speech in any vernacular—and Wee Willie Winkie had a colloquial acquaintance with three—was easy to the boy who could not yet manage his 'r's' and 'th's' aright.

Another man joined the conference, crying: 'O foolish men! What this babe says is true. He is the heart's heart of those white troops. For the sake of peace let them go both, for if he be taken, the regiment will break loose and gut the valley. Our villages are in the valley, and we shall not escape. That regiment are devils. They broke Khoda Yar's breastbone with kicks when he tried to take the rifles; and if we touch this child they will fire and rape and plunder for a month, till nothing remains. Better to send a man back to take the message and get a reward. I say that this child is their God, and that they will spare none of us, nor our women, if we harm him.'

It was Din Mahommed, the dismissed groom of the Colonel, who made the diversion, and an angry and heated discussion followed. Wee Willie Winkie, standing over Miss Allardyce, waited the upshot. Surely his 'Wegiment,' his own 'Wegiment,' would not desert him if they knew of his extremity.

The riderless pony brought the news to the 195th, though there had been consternation in the Colonel's household for an hour before. The little beast came in through the parade-ground in front of the main barracks, where the men were settling down to play Spoil-five till the afternoon. Devlin, the Colour-Sergeant of E Company, glanced at the empty saddle and tumbled through the barrack-rooms, kicking up each Room Corporal as he passed. 'Up, ye beggars! There's something happened to the Colonel's son,' he shouted.

'He couldn't fall off! S'elp me, 'e couldn't fall off,' blubbered a drummer-boy. 'Go an' hunt acrost the river. He's over there if he's anywhere, an' maybe those Pathans have got 'im. For the love o' Gawd don't look for 'im in the nullahs! Let's go over the river.'

'There's sense in Mott yet,' said Devlin. 'E Company, double out to the river—sharp!'

So E Company, in its shirt-sleeves mainly, doubled for the dear life, and in the rear toiled the perspiring Sergeant, adjuring it to double yet faster. The cantonment was alive with the men of the 195th hunting for Wee Willie Winkie, and the Colonel finally overtook E Company, far too exhausted to swear, struggling in the pebbles of the river-bed.

Up the hill under which Wee Willie Winkie's Bad Men were discussing the wisdom of carrying off the child and the girl, a look-out fired two shots.

'What have I said?' shouted Din Mahommed. 'There is the warning! The pulton are out already and are coming across the plain! Get away! Let us not be seen with the boy.'

The men waited for an instant, and then, as another shot was fired, withdrew into the hills, silently as they had appeared.

'Ve Wegiment is coming,' said Wee Willie Winkie confidently to Miss Allardyce, 'and it's all wight. Don't cwy!'

He needed the advice himself, for ten minutes later, when his father came up, he was weeping bitterly with his head in Miss Allardyce's lap.

And the men of the 195th carried him home with shouts and rejoicings; and Coppy, who had ridden a horse into a lather, met him, and, to his intense disgust, kissed him openly in the presence of the men.

But there was balm for his dignity. His father assured him that not only would the breaking of arrest be condoned, but that the good-conduct badge would be restored as soon as his mother could sew it on his blouse-sleeve. Miss Allardyce had told the Colonel a story that made him proud of his son.

'She belonged to you, Coppy,' said Wee Willie Winkie, indicating Miss Allardyce with a grimy forefinger. 'I knew she didn't ought to go acwoss ve wiver, and I knew ve Wegiment would come to me if I sent Jack home.'

'You're a hero, Winkie,' said Coppy—'a pukka hero!'

'I don't know what vat means,' said Wee Willie Winkie, 'but you mustn't call me Winkie any no more. I'm Percival Will'am Will'ams.'

And in this manner did Wee Willie Winkie enter into his manhood.

BAA BAA, BLACK SHEEP

The First Bag

When I was in my father's house, I was in a better place.

They were putting Punch to bed—the ayah and the hamal and Meeta, the big Surti boy, with the red-and-gold turban. Judy, already tucked inside her mosquito-curtains, was nearly asleep. Punch had been allowed to stay up for dinner. Many privileges had been accorded to Punch within the last ten days, and a greater kindness from the people of his world had encompassed his ways and works, which were mostly obstreperous. He sat on the edge of his bed and swung his bare legs defiantly.

'Punch-baba going to bye-lo?' said the ayah suggestively.

'No,' said Punch. 'Punch-baba wants the story about the Ranee that was turned into a tiger. Meeta must tell it, and the hamal shall hide behind the door and make tiger-noises at the proper time.'

'But Judy-baba will wake up,' said the ayah.

'Judy-baba is waked,' piped a small voice from the mosquito-curtains. 'There was a Ranee that lived at Delhi. Go on, Meeta,' and she fell fast asleep again while Meeta began the story.

Never had Punch secured the telling of that tale with so little opposition. He reflected for a long time. The hamal made the tiger-noises in twenty different keys.

''Top!' said Punch authoritatively. 'Why doesn't Papa come in and say he is going to give me put-put?'

'Punch-baba is going away,' said the ayah. 'In another week there will be no Punch-baba to pull my hair any more.' She sighed softly, for the boy of the household was very dear to her heart.

'Up the Ghauts in a train?' said Punch, standing on his bed. 'All the way to Nassick where the Ranee-Tiger lives?'

'Not to Nassick this year, little Sahib,' said Meeta, lifting him on his shoulder. 'Down to the sea where the coconuts are thrown, and across the sea in a big ship. Will you take Meeta with you to Belait?'

'You shall all come,' said Punch, from the height of Meeta's strong arms. 'Meeta and the ayah and the hamal and Bhini-in-the-Garden, and the salaam-Captain-Sahib-snake-man.'

There was no mockery in Meeta's voice when he replied: 'Great is the Sahib's favour,' and laid the little man down in the bed, while the ayah, sitting in the moonlight at the doorway, lulled him to sleep with an interminable canticle such as they sing in the Roman Catholic Church at Parel. Punch curled himself into a ball and slept.

Next morning Judy shouted that there was a rat in the nursery, and thus he forgot to tell her the wonderful news. It did not much matter, for Judy was only three and she would not have understood. But Punch was five; and he knew that going to England would be much nicer than a trip to Nassick.

Papa and Mamma sold the brougham and the piano, and stripped the house, and curtailed the allowance of crockery for the daily meals, and took long counsel together over a bundle of letters bearing the Rocklington postmark.

'The worst of it is that one can't be certain of anything,' said Papa, pulling his moustache. 'The letters in themselves are excellent, and the terms are moderate enough.'

'The worst of it is that the children will grow up away from me,' thought Mamma; but she did not say it aloud.

'We are only one case among hundreds,' said Papa bitterly. 'You shall go Home again in five years, dear.'

'Punch will be ten then—and Judy eight. Oh, how long and long and long the time will be! And we have to leave them among strangers.'

'Punch is a cheery little chap. He's sure to make friends wherever he goes.'

'And who could help loving my Ju?'

They were standing over the cots in the nursery late at night, and I think that Mamma was crying softly. After Papa had gone away, she knelt down by the side of Judy's cot. The ayah saw her and put up a prayer that the Memsahib might never find the love of her children taken away from her and given to a stranger.

Mamma's own prayer was a slightly illogical one. Summarised it ran: 'Let strangers love my children and be as good to them as I should be, but let me preserve their love and their confidence for ever and ever. Amen.' Punch scratched himself in his sleep, and Judy moaned a little.

Next day they all went down to the sea, and there was a scene at the Apollo Bunder when Punch discovered that Meeta could not come too, and Judy learned that the ayah must be left behind. But Punch found a thousand fascinating things in the rope, block, and steam-pipe line on the big P. & O. steamer long before Meeta and the ayah had dried their tears.

'Come back, Punch-baba,' said the ayah. 'Come back,' said Meeta, 'and be a Burra Sahib.'

'Yes,' said Punch, lifted up in his father's arms to wave good-bye. 'Yes, I will come back, and I will be a Burra Sahib Bahadur!'

At the end of the first day Punch demanded to be set down in England, which he was certain must be close at hand. Next day there was a merry breeze, and Punch was very sick. 'When I come back to Bombay,' said Punch on his recovery, 'I will come by the road—in a broom-gharri. This is a very naughty ship.'

The Swedish boatswain consoled him, and he modified his opinions as the voyage went on. There was so much to see and to handle and ask questions about that Punch nearly forgot the ayah and Meeta and the hamal, and with difficulty remembered a few words of the Hindustani once his second speech.

But Judy was much worse. The day before the steamer reached Southampton, Mamma asked her if she would not like to see the ayah again. Judy's blue eyes turned to the stretch of sea that had. swallowed all her tiny past, and she said 'Ayah! What ayah?'

Mamma cried over her and Punch marvelled. It was then that he heard for the first time Mamma's passionate appeal to him never to let Judy forget Mamma. Seeing that Judy was young, ridiculously young, and that Mamma, every evening for four weeks past, had come into the cabin to sing her and

Punch to sleep with a mysterious rune that he called 'Sonny, my soul,' Punch could not understand what Mamma meant. But he strove to do his duty; for, the moment Mamma left the cabin, he said to Judy: 'Ju, you bemember Mamma?'

''Torse I do,' said Judy.

'Then always bemember Mamma, 'r else I won't give you the paper ducks that the red-haired Captain Sahib cut out for me.'

So Judy promised always to 'bemember Mamma.'

Many and many a time was Mamma's command laid upon Punch, and Papa would say the same thing with an insistence that awed the child.

'You must make haste and learn to write, Punch,' said Papa, 'and then you'll be able to write letters to us in Bombay.'

'I'll come into your room,' said Punch, and Papa choked.

Papa and Mamma were always choking in those days. If Punch took Judy to task for not 'bemembering,' they choked. If Punch sprawled on the sofa in the Southampton lodging-house and sketched his future in purple and gold, they choked; and so they did if Judy put up her mouth for a kiss.

Through many days all four were vagabonds on the face of the earth—Punch with no one to give orders to, Judy too young for anything, and Papa and Mamma grave, distracted, and choking.

'Where,' demanded Punch, wearied of a loathsome contrivance on four wheels with a mound of luggage atop—'where is our broom-gharri? This thing talks so much that I can't talk. Where is our own broom-gharri? When I was at Bandstand before we comed away, I asked Inverarity Sahib why he was sitting in it, and he said it was his own. And I said, "I will give it you"—I like Inverarity Sahib—and I said, "Can you put your legs through the pully-wag loops by the windows?" And Inverarity Sahib said No, and laughed. 'I can put my legs through the pully-wag loops. I can put my legs through these pully-wag loops. Look! Oh, Mamma's crying again! I didn't know I wasn't not to do so.'

Punch drew his legs out of the loops of the four-wheeler: the door opened and he slid to the earth, in a cascade of parcels, at the door of an austere little villa whose gates bore the legend 'Downe Lodge.' Punch gathered himself together and eyed the house with disfavour. It stood on a sandy road, and a cold wind tickled his knickerbockered legs.

'Let us go away,' said Punch. 'This is not a pretty place.'

But Mamma and Papa and Judy had left the cab, and all the luggage was being taken into the house. At the doorstep stood a woman in black, and she smiled largely, with dry chapped lips. Behind her was a man, big, bony, grey, and lame as to one leg—behind him a boy of twelve, blackhaired and oily in appearance. Punch surveyed the trio, and advanced without fear, as he had been accustomed to do in Bombay when callers came and he happened to be playing in the veranda.

'How do you do?' said he. 'I am Punch.' But they were all looking at the luggage—all except the grey man, who shook hands with Punch, and said he was 'a smart little fellow.' There was much running about and banging of boxes, and Punch curled himself up on the sofa in the dining-room and considered things.

'I don't like these people,' said Punch. 'But never mind. We'll go away soon. We have always went away soon from everywhere. I wish we was gone back to Bombay soon.'

The wish bore no fruit. For six days Mamma wept at intervals, and showed the woman in black all Punch's clothes—a liberty which Punch resented. 'But p'raps she's a new white ayah,' he thought. 'I'm to call her Antirosa, but she doesn't call me Sahib. She says just Punch,' he confided to Judy. 'What is Antirosa?'

Judy didn't know. Neither she nor Punch had heard anything of an animal called an aunt. Their world had been Papa and Mamma, who knew everything, permitted everything, and loved everybody—even Punch when he used to go into the garden at Bombay and fill his nails with mould after the weekly nail-cutting, because, as he explained between two strokes of the slipper to his sorely-tried father, his fingers 'felt so new at the ends.'

In an undefined way Punch judged it advisable to keep both parents between himself and the woman in black and the boy with black hair. He did not approve of them. He liked the grey man, who had expressed a wish to be called 'Uncle-harri.' They nodded at each other when they met, and the grey man showed him a little ship with rigging that took up and down.

'She is a model of the Brisk—the little Brisk that was sore exposed that day at Navarino.' The grey man hummed the last words and fell into a reverie. 'I'll tell you about Navarino, Punch, when we go for walks together; and you mustn't touch the ship, because she's the Brisk.'

Long before that walk, 'the first of many, was taken, they roused Punch and Judy in the chill dawn of a February morning to say Good-bye; and of all people in the wide earth to Papa and Mamma—both crying this time. Punch was very sleepy and Judy was cross.

'Don't forget us,' pleaded Mamma. 'Oh, my little son, don't forget us, and see that Judy remembers too.'

'I've told Judy to bemember,' said Punch, wriggling, for his father's beard tickled his neck. 'I've told Judy—ten—forty—'leven thousand times. But Ju's so young—quite a baby—isn't she?'

'Yes,' said Papa, 'quite a baby, and you must be good to Judy, and make haste to learn to write and—and—and—'

Punch was back in his bed again. Judy was fast asleep, and there was the rattle of a cab below. Papa and Mamma had gone away. Not to Nassick; that was across the sea. To some place much nearer, of course, and equally of course they would return. They came back after dinner-parties, and Papa had come back after he had been to a place called 'The Snows,' and Mamma with him, to Punch and Judy at Mrs. Inverarity's house in Marine Lines. Assuredly they would come back again. So Punch fell asleep till the true morning, when the black-haired boy met him with the information that Papa and Mamma had gone to Bombay, and that he and Judy were to stay at Downe Lodge 'for ever.' Antirosa, tearfully appealed to for a contradiction, said that Harry had spoken the truth, and that it behoved Punch to fold up his clothes neatly on going to bed. Punch went out and wept bitterly with Judy, into whose fair head he had driven some ideas of the meaning of separation.

When a matured man discovers that he has been deserted by Providence, deprived of his God, and cast without help, comfort, or sympathy, upon a world which is new and strange to him, his despair, which may find expression in evil living, the writing of his experiences, or the more satisfactory diversion of suicide, is generally supposed to be impressive. A child, under exactly similar circumstances as far as its knowledge goes, cannot very well curse God and die. It howls till its nose is red, its eyes are sore, and its head aches. Punch and Judy, through no fault of their own, had lost all their world. They sat in the hall and cried; the black-haired boy looking on from afar.

The model of the ship availed nothing, though the grey man assured Punch that he might pull the rigging up and down as much as he pleased; and Judy was promised free entry into the kitchen. They wanted Papa and Mamma, gone to Bombay beyond the seas, and their grief while it lasted was without remedy.

When the tears ceased the house was very still. Antirosa had decided that it was better to let the children 'have their cry out,' and the boy had gone to school. Punch raised his head from the floor and sniffed mournfully. Judy was nearly asleep. Three short years had not taught her how to bear sorrow with full knowledge. There was a distant, dull boom in the air—a repeated heavy thud. Punch knew that sound in Bombay in the monsoon. It was the sea—the sea that must be traversed before any one could get to Bombay.

'Quick, Ju!' he cried. 'We're close to the sea. I can hear it! Listen! That's where they've went. P'raps we can catch them if we was in time. They didn't mean to go without us. They've only forgot.'

'Iss,' said Judy. 'They've only forgotted. Less go to the sea.'

The hall-door was open and so was the garden-gate.

'It's very, very big, this place,' he said, looking cautiously down the road, 'and we will get lost. But I will find a man and order him to take me back to my house—like I did in Bombay.'

He took Judy by the hand, and the two ran hatless in the direction of the sound of the sea. Downe Lodge was almost the last of a range of newly-built houses running out, through a field of brick-mounds, to a heath where gipsies occasionally camped and where the Garrison Artillery of Rocklington practised. There were few people to be seen, and the children might have been taken for those of the soldiery who ranged far. Half an hour the wearied little-legs tramped across heath, potato-patch, and sand-dune.

'I'se so tired,' said Judy; 'and Mamma will be angry.'

'Mamma's never angry. I suppose she is waiting at the sea now while Papa gets tickets. We'll find them and go along with them. Ju, you mustn't sit down. Only a little more and we'll come to the sea. Ju, if you sit down I'll thmack you!' said Punch.

They climbed another dune, and came upon the great grey sea at low tide. Hundreds of crabs were scuttling about the beach, but there was no trace of Papa and Mamma, not even of a ship upon the waters—nothing but sand and mud for miles and miles.

And 'Uncleharri' found them by chance—very muddy and very forlorn—Punch dissolved in tears, but trying to divert Judy with an 'ickle trab,' and Judy wailing to the pitiless horizon for 'Mamma, Mamma!'—and again 'Mamma!'

The Second Bag

Ah, well-a-day, for we are souls bereaved!
Of all the creatures under Heaven's wide cope
We are most hopeless, who had once most hope,
And most beliefless, who had most believed.
A.H. Clough.

All this time not a word about Black Sheep. He came later, and Harry, the black-haired boy, was mainly responsible for his coming.

Judy—who could help loving little Judy?—passed, by special permit, into the kitchen and thence straight to Aunty Rosa's heart. Harry was Aunty Rosa's one child, and Punch was the extra boy about the house. There was no special place for him or his little affairs, and he was forbidden to sprawl on sofas and explain his ideas about the manufacture of this world and his hopes for his future. Sprawling was lazy and wore out sofas, and little boys were not expected to talk. They were talked to, and the talking-to was intended for the benefit of their morals. As the unquestioned despot of the house at Bombay, Punch could not quite understand how he came to be of no account in this his new life.

Harry might reach across the table and take what he wanted; Judy might point and get what she wanted. Punch was forbidden to do either. The grey man was his great hope and stand-by for many months after Mamma and Papa left, and he had forgotten to tell Judy to 'bemember Mamma.'

This lapse was excusable, because in the interval he had been introduced by Aunty Rosa to two very impressive things—an abstraction called God, the intimate friend and ally of Aunty Rosa, generally believed to live behind the kitchen-range because it was hot there—and a dirty brown book filled with unintelligible dots and marks. Punch was always anxious to oblige everybody. He therefore welded the story of the Creation on to what he could recollect of his Indian fairy tales, and scandalised Aunty Rosa by repeating the result to Judy. It was a sin, a grievous sin, and Punch was talked to for a quarter of an hour. He could not understand where the iniquity came in, but was careful not to repeat the offence, because Aunty Rosa told him that God had heard every word he had said and was very angry. If this were true why didn't God come and say so, thought Punch, and dismissed the matter from his mind. Afterwards he learned to know the Lord as the only thing in the world more awful than Aunty Rosa—as a Creature that stood in the background and counted the strokes of the cane.

But the reading was, just then, a much more serious matter than any creed. Aunty Rosa sat him upon a table and told him that A B meant ab.

'Why?' said Punch. 'A is a and B is bee. Why does A B mean ab? '

'Because I tell you it does,' said Aunty Rosa, 'and you've got to say it.'

Punch said it accordingly, and for a month, hugely against his will, stumbled through the brown book, not in the least comprehending what it meant. But Uncle Harry, who walked much and generally alone, was wont to come into the nursery and suggest to Aunty Rosa that Punch should walk with him. He seldom spoke, but he showed Punch all Rocklington, from the mud-banks and the sand of the back-bay to the great harbours where ships lay at anchor, and the dockyards where the hammers were never still, and the marine-store shops, and the shiny brass counters in the Offices where Uncle Harry went once every three months with a slip of blue paper and received sovereigns in exchange; for he held a wound-pension. Punch heard, too, from his lips the story of the battle of Navarino, where the sailors of the Fleet, for three days afterwards, were deaf as posts and could only sign to each other. 'That was because of the noise of the guns,' said Uncle Harry, 'and I have got the wadding of a bullet somewhere inside me now.'

Punch regarded him with curiosity. He had not the least idea what wadding was, and his notion of a bullet was a dockyard cannon-ball bigger than his own head. How could Uncle Harry keep a cannon-ball inside him? He was afraid to ask, for fear Uncle Harry might be angry.

Punch had never known what anger—real anger—meant until one terrible day when Harry had taken his paint-box to paint a boat with, and Punch had protested. Then Uncle Harry had appeared on the scene and, muttering something about 'strangers' children,' had with a stick smitten the black-haired boy across the shoulders till he wept and yelled, and Aunty Rosa came in and abused Uncle Harry for cruelty to his own flesh and blood, and Punch shuddered to the tips of his shoes. 'It wasn't my fault,' he explained to the boy, but both Harry and Aunty Rosa said that it was, and that Punch had told tales, and for a week there were no more walks with Uncle Harry.

But that week brought a great joy to Punch.

He had repeated till he was thrice weary the statement that 'The Cat lay on the Mat and the Rat came in.'

'Now I can truly read,' said Punch, 'and now I will never read anything in the world.'

He put the brown book in the cupboard where his school-books lived and accidentally tumbled out a venerable volume, without covers, labelled Sharpe's Magazine. There was the most portentous picture of a Griffin on the first page, with verses below. The Griffin carried off one sheep a day from a German village, till a man came with a 'falchion 'and split the Griffin open. Goodness only knew what a falchion was, but there was the Griffin and his history was an improvement upon the eternal Cat.

'This,' said Punch, 'means things, and now I will know all about everything in all the world.' He read till the light failed, not understanding a tithe of the meaning,. but tantalised by glimpses of new worlds hereafter to be revealed.

'What is a "falchion"? What is a "e-wee lamb"? What is a "base ussurper"? What is a "verdant mead"?' he demanded, with flushed cheeks, at bedtime, of the astonished Aunty Rosa.

'Say your prayers and go to sleep,' she replied, and that was all the help Punch then or afterwards found at her hands in the new and delightful exercise of reading.

'Aunty Rosa only knows about God and things like that,' argued Punch. 'Uncle Harry will tell me.'

The next walk proved that Uncle Harry could not help either; but he allowed Punch to talk, and even sat down on a bench to hear about the Griffin. Other walks brought other stories as Punch ranged farther afield, for the house held large store of old books that no one ever opened—from Frank Fairlegh in serial numbers, and the earlier poems of Tennyson, contributed anonymously to Sharpe's Magazine, to '62 Exhibition Catalogues, gay with colours and delightfully incomprehensible, and odd leaves of Gulliver's Travels.

As soon as Punch could string a few pot-hooks together he wrote to Bombay, demanding by return of post 'all the books in all the world'. Papa could not comply with this modest indent, but sent Grimm's Fairy Tales and a Hans Andersen. That was enough. If he were only left alone Punch could pass, at any hour he chose, into a land of his own, beyond reach of Aunty Rosa and her God, Harry and his teasements, and Judy's claims to be played with.

'Don't disturve me, I'm reading. Go and play in the kitchen,' grunted Punch. 'Aunty Rosa lets you go there.' Judy was cutting her second teeth and was fretful. She appealed to Aunty Rosa, who descended on Punch.

'I was reading,' he explained, 'reading a book. I want to read.'

'You're only doing that to show off,' said Aunty Rosa. 'But we'll see. Play with Judy now, and don't open a book for a week.'

Judy did not pass a very enjoyable playtime with Punch, who was consumed with indignation. There was a pettiness at the bottom of the prohibition which puzzled him.

'It's what I like to do,' he said, 'and she's found out that and stopped me. Don't cry, Ju—it wasn't your fault—please don't cry, or she'll say I made you.'

Ju loyally mopped up her tears, and the two played in their nursery, a room in the basement and half underground, to which they were regularly sent after the mid-day dinner while Aunty Rosa slept. She drank wine—that is to say, something from a bottle in the cellaret—for her stomach's sake, but if she did not fall asleep she would sometimes come into the nursery to see that the children were really playing. Now bricks, wooden hoops, ninepins, and chinaware cannot amuse for ever, especially when all Fairyland is to be won by the mere opening of a book, and, as often as not, Punch would be discovered reading to Judy or telling her interminable tales. That was an offence in the eyes of the law, and Judy would be whisked off by Aunty Rosa, while Punch was left to play alone, 'and be sure that I hear you doing it.'

It was not a cheering employ, for he had to make a playful noise. At last, with infinite craft, he devised an arrangement whereby the table could be supported as to three legs on toy bricks, leaving the fourth clear to bring down on the floor. He could work the table with one hand and hold the book with the other. This he did till an evil day when Aunty Rosa pounced upon him unawares and told him that he was 'acting a lie.'

'If you're old enough to do that,' she said—her temper was always worst after dinner—'you're old enough to be beaten.'

'But—I'm—I'm not a animal!' said Punch aghast. He remembered Uncle Harry and the stick, and turned white. Aunty Rosa had hidden a light cane behind her, and Punch was beaten then and there over the shoulders. It was a revelation to him. The room-door was shut, and he was left to weep himself into repentance and work out his own gospel of life.

Aunty Rosa, he argued, had the power to beat him with many stripes. It was unjust and cruel, and Mamma and Papa would never have allowed it. Unless perhaps, as Aunty Rosa seemed to imply, they had sent secret orders. In which case he was abandoned indeed. It would be discreet in the future to propitiate Aunty Rosa, but then again, even in matters in which he was innocent, he had been accused of wishing to 'show off.' He had 'shown off' before visitors when he had attacked a strange gentleman—Harry's uncle, not his own—with requests for information about the Griffin and the falchion, and the precise nature of the Tilbury in which Frank Fairlegh rode—all points of paramount interest which he was bursting to understand. Clearly it would not do to pretend to care for Aunty Rosa.

At this point Harry entered and stood afar off, eyeing Punch, a dishevelled heap in the corner of the room, with disgust.

'You're a liar—a young liar,' said Harry, with great unction, 'and you're to have tea down here because you're not fit to speak to us. And you're not to speak to Judy again till Mother gives you leave. You'll corrupt her. You're only fit to associate with the servant. Mother says so.'

Having reduced Punch to a second agony of tears, Harry departed upstairs with the news that Punch was still rebellious.

Uncle Harry sat uneasily in the dining-room. 'Damn it all, Rosa,' said he at last, 'can't you leave the child alone? He's a good enough little chap when I meet him.'

'He puts on his best manners with you, Henry,' said Aunty Rosa, 'but I'm afraid, I'm very much afraid, that he is the Black Sheep of the family.'

Harry heard and stored up the name for future use. Judy cried till she was bidden to stop, her brother not being worth tears; and the evening concluded with the return of Punch to the upper regions and a private sitting at which all the blinding horrors of Hell were revealed to Punch with such store of imagery as Aunty Rosa's narrow mind possessed.

Most grievous of all was Judy's round eyed reproach, and Punch went to bed in the depths of the Valley of Humiliation. He shared his room with Harry and knew the torture in store. For an hour and a half he had to answer that young gentleman's questions as to his motives for telling a lie, and a grievous lie, the precise quantity of punishment inflicted by Aunty Rosa, and had also to profess his deep gratitude for such religious instruction as Harry thought fit to impart.

From that day began the downfall of Punch, now Black Sheep.

'Untrustworthy in one thing, untrustworthy in all,' said Aunty Rosa, and Harry felt that Black Sheep was delivered into his hands. He would wake him up in the night to ask him why he was such a liar.

'I don't know,' Punch would reply.

'Then don't you think you ought to get up and pray to God for a new heart?'

'Y-yess.'

'Get out and pray, then!' And Punch would get out of bed with raging hate in his heart against all the world, seen and unseen. He was always tumbling into trouble. Harry had a knack of cross-examining him as to his day's doings, which seldom failed to lead him, sleepy and savage, into half-a-dozen contradictions—all duly reported to Aunty Rosa next morning.

'But it wasn't a lie,' Punch would begin, charging into a laboured explanation that landed him more hopelessly in the mire. 'I said that I didn't say my prayers twice over in the day, and that was on Tuesday. Once I did. I know I did, but Harry said I didn't,' and so forth, till the tension brought tears, and he was dismissed from the table in disgrace.

'You usen't to be as bad as this,' said Judy, awestricken at the catalogue of Black Sheep's crimes. 'Why are you so bad now?'

'I don't know,' Black Sheep would reply. 'I'm not, if I only wasn't bothered upside-down. I knew what I did, and I want to say so but Harry always makes it out different somehow, and Aunty Rosa doesn't believe a word I say. Oh, Ju! Don't you say I'm bad too.'

'Aunty Rosa says you are,' said Judy. 'She told the Vicar so when he came yesterday.'

'Why does she tell all the people outside the house about me? It isn't fair,' said Black Sheep. 'When I was in Bombay, and was bad—doing bad, not made-up bad like this—Mamma told Papa, and Papa told me he knew, and that was all. Outside people didn't know too—even Meeta didn't know.'

'I don't remember,' said Judy wistfully. 'I was all little then. Mamma was just as fond of you as she was of me, wasn't she?'

''Course she was. So was Papa. So was everybody.'

'Aunty Rosa likes me more than she does you. She says that you are a Trial and a Black Sheep, and I'm not to speak to you more than I can help.'

'Always? Not outside of the times when you mustn't speak to me at all?'

Judy nodded her head mournfully. Black Sheep turned away in despair, but Judy's arms were round his neck.

'Never mind, Punch,' she whispered. 'I will speak to you just the same as ever and ever. You're my own own brother though you are—though Aunty Rosa says you're bad, and Harry says you are a little coward. He says that if I pulled your hair hard, you'd cry.'

'Pull, then,' said Punch.

Judy pulled gingerly.

'Pull harder—as hard as you can! There! I don't mind how much you pull it now. If you'll speak to me same as ever I'll let you pull it as much as you like—pull it out if you like. But I know if Harry came and stood by and made you do it I'd cry.'

So the two children sealed the compact with a kiss, and Black Sheep's heart was cheered within him, and by extreme caution and careful avoidance of Harry he acquired virtue, and was allowed to read undisturbed for a week. Uncle Harry took him for walks, and consoled him with rough tenderness, never calling him Black Sheep. 'It's good for you, I suppose, Punch,' he used to say. 'Let us sit down. I'm getting tired.' His steps led him now not to the beach, but to the Cemetery of Rocklington, amid the potato-fields. For hours the grey man would sit on a tombstone, while Black Sheep would read epitaphs, and then with a sigh would stump home again.

'I shall lie there soon,' said he to Black Sheep, one winter evening, when his face showed white as a worn silver coin under the light of the lych gate. 'You needn't tell Aunty Rosa.'

A month later he turned sharp round, ere half a morning walk was completed, and stumped back to the house. 'Put me to bed, Rosa,' he muttered. 'I've walked my last. The wadding has found me out.'

They put him to bed, and for a fortnight the shadow of his sickness lay upon the. house, and Black Sheep went to and fro unobserved. Papa had sent him some new books, and he was told to keep quiet. He retired into his own world, and was perfectly happy. Even at night his felicity was unbroken. He could lie in bed and string himself tales of travel and adventure while Harry was downstairs.

'Uncle Harry's going to die,' said Judy, who now lived almost entirely with Aunty Rosa.

'I'm very sorry,' said Black Sheep soberly. 'He told me that a long time ago.'

Aunty Rosa heard the conversation. 'Will nothing check your wicked tongue? 'she said angrily. There were blue circles round her eyes.

Black Sheep retreated to the nursery and read Cometh up as a Flower with deep and uncomprehending interest. He had been forbidden to open it on account of its 'sinfulness,' but the bonds of the Universe were crumbling, and Aunty Rosa was in great grief.

'I'm glad,' said Black Sheep. 'She's unhappy now. It wasn't a lie, though. I knew. He told me not to tell.'

That night Black Sheep woke with a start. Harry was not in the room, and there was a sound of sobbing on the next floor. Then the voice of Uncle Harry, singing the song of the Battle of Navarino, came through the darkness:—

'Our vanship was the Asia—
The Albion and Genoa!'

'He's getting well,' thought Black Sheep, who knew the song through all its seventeen verses. But the blood froze at his little heart as he thought. The voice leapt an octave, and ran shrill as a boatswain's pipe:—

'And next came on the lovely Rose,

The Philomel, her fire-ship, closed,
And the little Brisk was sore exposed
That day at Navarino.'

'That day at Navarino, Uncle Harry! 'shouted Black Sheep, half wild with excitement and fear of he knew not what.

A door opened, and Aunty Rosa screamed up the staircase: 'Hush! For God's sake hush, you little devil! Uncle Harry is dead!'

The Third Bag

Journeys end in lovers' meeting,
very wise man's son doth know.

'I wonder what will happen to me now,' thought Black Sheep, when semi-pagan rites peculiar to the burial of the Dead in middle-class houses had been accomplished, and Aunty Rosa, awful in black crape, had returned to this life. 'I don't think I've done anything bad that she knows of. I suppose I will soon. She will be very cross after Uncle Harry's dying, and Harry will be cross too. I'll keep in the nursery.'

Unfortunately for Punch's plans, it was decided that he should be sent to a day-school which Harry attended. This meant a morning walk with Harry, and perhaps an evening one; but the prospect of freedom in the interval was refreshing. 'Harry'll tell everything I do, but I won't do anything,' said Black Sheep. Fortified with this virtuous resolution, he went to school only to find that Harry's version of his character had preceded him, and that life was a burden in consequence. He took stock of his associates. Some of them were unclean, some of them talked in dialect, many dropped their h's, and there were two Jews and a negro, or some one quite as dark, in the assembly. 'That's a hubshi,' said Black Sheep to himself. 'Even Meeta used to laugh at a hubshi. I don't think this is a proper place.' He was indignant for at least an hour, till he reflected that any expostulation on his part would be by Aunty Rosa construed into 'showing off,' and that Harry would tell the boys.

'How do you like school?' said Aunty Rosa at the end of the day.

'I think it is a very nice place,' said Punch quietly.

'I suppose you warned the boys of Black Sheep's character? 'said Aunty Rosa to Harry.

'Oh yes,' said the censor of Black Sheep's morals. 'They know all about him.'

'If I was with my father,' said Black Sheep, stung to the quick, 'I shouldn't speak to those boys. He wouldn't let me. They live in shops. I saw them go into shops—where their fathers live and sell things.'

'You're too good for that school, are you?' said Aunty Rosa, with a bitter smile. 'You ought to be grateful, Black Sheep, that those boys speak to you at all. It isn't every school that takes little liars.'

Harry did not fail to make much capital out of Black Sheep's ill-considered remark; with the result that several boys, including the hubshi, demonstrated to Black Sheep the eternal equality of the human race by smacking his head, and his consolation from Aunty Rosa was that it 'served him right for being vain.' He learned, however, to keep his opinions to himself, and by propitiating Harry in carrying books and the like to get a little peace. His existence was not too joyful. From nine till twelve he was at school, and from two to four, except on Saturdays. In the evenings he was sent down into the nursery to prepare his lessons for the next day, and every night came the dreaded cross-questionings at Harry's hand. Of Judy he saw but little. She was deeply religious—at six years of age Religion is easy to come by—and sorely divided between her natural love for Black Sheep and her love for Aunty Rosa, who could do no wrong.

The lean woman returned that love with interest, and Judy, when she dared, took advantage of this for the remission of Black Sheep's penalties. Failures in lessons at school were punished at home by a week without reading other than schoolbooks, and Harry brought the news of such a failure with glee. Further, Black Sheep was then bound to repeat his lessons at bedtime to Harry, who generally succeeded in making him break down, and consoled him by gloomiest forebodings for the morrow. Harry was at once spy, practical joker, inquisitor, and Aunty Rosa's deputy executioner. He filled his many posts to admiration. From his actions, now that Uncle Harry was dead, there was no appeal. Black Sheep had not been permitted to keep any self-respect at school: at home he was, of course, utterly discredited, and grateful for any pity that the servant-girls—they changed frequently at Downe Lodge because they, too, were liars—might show. 'You're just fit to row in the same boat with Black Sheep,' was a sentiment that each new Jane or Eliza might expect to hear, before a month was over, from Aunty Rosa's lips; and Black Sheep was used to ask new girls whether they had yet been compared to him. Harry was 'Master Harry' in their mouths; Judy was officially 'Miss Judy'; but Black Sheep was never anything more than Black Sheep tout court.

As time went on and the memory of Papa and Mamma became wholly overlaid by the unpleasant task of writing them letters, under Aunty Rosa's eye, each Sunday, Black Sheep forgot what manner of life he had led in the beginning of things. Even Judy's appeals to 'try and remember about Bombay' failed to quicken him.

'I can't remember,' he said. 'I know I used to give orders and Mamma kissed me.'

'Aunty Rosa will kiss you if you are good,' pleaded Judy.

'Ugh! I don't want to be kissed by Aunty Rosa. She'd say I was doing it to get something more to eat.'

The weeks lengthened into months, and the holidays came; but just before the holidays Black Sheep fell into deadly sin.

Among the many boys whom Harry had incited to 'punch Black Sheep's head because he daren't hit back,' was one more aggravating than the rest, who, in an unlucky moment, fell upon Black Sheep when Harry was not near. The blows stung, and Black Sheep struck back at random with all the power at his command. The bay dropped and whimpered. Black Sheep was astounded at his own act, but, feeling the unresisting body under him, shook it with both his hands in blind fury and then began to throttle his enemy; meaning honestly to slay him. There was a scuffle, and Black Sheep was torn off the body by Harry and some colleagues, and cuffed home tingling but exultant. Aunty Rosa was out. Pending her arrival, Harry set himself to lecture Black Sheep on the sin of murder—which he described as the offence of Cain.

'Why didn't you fight him fair? What did you hit him when he was down for, you little cur?'

Black Sheep looked up at Harry's throat and then at a knife on the dinner-table.

'I don't understand,' he said wearily. 'You always set him on me and told me I was a coward when I blubbed. Will you leave me alone until Aunty Rosa comes in? She'll beat me if you tell her I ought to be beaten; so it's all right.'

'It's all wrong,' said Harry magisterially. 'You nearly killed him, and I shouldn't wonder if he dies.'

'Will he die?' said Black Sheep.

'I daresay,' said Harry, 'and then you'll be hanged, and go to Hell.'

'All right,' said Black Sheep, picking up the table-knife. 'Then I'll kill you now. You say things and do things and—and I don't know how things happen, and you never leave me alone—and I don't care what happens!'

He ran at the boy with the knife, and Harry fled upstairs to his room, promising Black Sheep the finest thrashing in the world when Aunty Rosa returned. Black Sheep sat at the bottom of the stairs, the table-knife in his hand, and wept for that he had not killed Harry. The servant-girl came up from the kitchen, took the knife away, and consoled him. But Black Sheep was beyond consolation. He would be badly beaten by Aunty Rosa; then there would be another beating at Harry's hands; then Judy would not be allowed to speak to him; then the tale would be told at school, and then—

There was no one to help and no one to care, and the best way out of the business was by death. A knife would hurt, but Aunty Rosa had told him, a year ago, that if he sucked paint he would die. He went into the nursery, unearthed the now disused Noah's Ark, and sucked the paint off as many animals as remained. It tasted abominably, but he had licked Noah's Dove clean by the time Aunty Rosa and Judy returned. He went upstairs and greeted them with: 'Please, Aunty Rosa, I believe I've nearly killed a boy at school, and I've tried to kill Harry, and when you've done all about God and Hell, will you beat me and get it over?'

The tale of the assault as told by Harry could only be explained on the ground of possession by the Devil. Wherefore Black Sheep was not only most excellently beaten, once by Aunty Rosa, and once, when thoroughly cowed down, by Harry, but he was further prayed for at family prayers, together with Jane, who had stolen a cold rissole from the pantry, and snuffled audibly as her sin was brought before the Throne of Grace. Black Sheep was sore and stiff but triumphant. He would die that very night and be rid of them all. No, he would ask for no forgiveness from Harry, and at bed-time would stand no questioning at Harry's hands, even though addressed as 'Young Cain.'

'I've been beaten,' said he, 'and I've done other things. I don't care what I do. If you speak to me to-night, Harry, I'll get out and try to kill you. Now you can kill me if you like.'

Harry took his bed into the spare room, and Black Sheep lay down to die.

It may be that the makers of Noah's Arks know that their animals are likely to find their way into young mouths, and paint them accordingly. Certain it is that the common, weary next morning broke through the windows and found Black Sheep quite well and a good deal ashamed of himself, but richer by the knowledge that he could, in extremity, secure himself against Harry for the future.

When he descended to breakfast on the first day of the holidays, he was greeted with the news that Harry, Aunty Rosa, and Judy were going away to Brighton, while Black Sheep was to stay in the house with the servant. His latest outbreak suited Aunty Rosa's plans admirably. It gave her good excuse for leaving the extra boy behind. Papa in Bombay, who really seemed to know a young sinner's wants to the hour, sent, that week, a package of new books. And with these, and the society of Jane on board-wages, Black Sheep was left alone for a month.

The books lasted for ten days. They were eaten too quickly in long gulps of twelve hours at a time. Then came days of doing absolutely nothing, of dreaming dreams and marching imaginary armies up and down stairs, of counting the number of banisters, and of measuring the length and breadth of every room in handspans—fifty down the side, thirty across, and fifty back again. Jane made many friends, and, after receiving Black Sheep's assurance that he would not tell of her absences, went out daily for long hours. Black Sheep would follow the rays of the sinking sun from the kitchen to the dining-room and thence upward to his own bedroom until all was grey dark, and he ran down to the kitchen fire and read by its light. He was happy in that he was left alone and could read as much as he pleased. But, later, he grew afraid of the shadows of window curtains and the flapping of doors and the creaking of shutters. He went out into the garden, and the rustling of the laurel-bushes frightened him.

He was glad when they all returned—Aunty Rosa, Harry, and Judy—full of news, and Judy laden with gifts. Who could help loving loyal little Judy? In return for all her merry babblement, Black Sheep confided to her that the distance from the hall-door to the top of the first landing was exactly one-hundred and eighty-four handspans. He had found it out himself!

Then the old life recommenced; but with a difference, and a new sin. To his other iniquities Black Sheep had now added a phenomenal clumsiness—was as unfit to trust in action as he was in word. He himself could not account for spilling everything he touched, upsetting glasses as he put his hand put, and bumping his head against doors that were manifestly shut. There was a grey haze upon all his world, and it narrowed month by month, until at last it left Black Sheep almost alone with the flapping curtains that were so like ghosts, and the nameless terrors of broad daylight that were only coats on pegs after all.

Holidays came and holidays went, and Black Sheep was taken to see many people whose faces were all exactly alike; was beaten when occasion demanded, and tortured by Harry on all possible occasions; but defended by Judy through good and evil report, though she hereby drew upon herself the wrath of Aunty Rosa,

The weeks were interminable and Papa and Mamma were clean forgotten. Harry had left school and was a clerk in a Banking-Office. Freed from his presence, Black Sheep resolved that he should no longer be deprived of his allowance of pleasure-reading. Consequently when he failed at school he reported that all was well, and conceived a large contempt for Aunty Rosa as he saw how easy it was to deceive her. 'She says I'm a little liar when I don't tell lies, and now I do, she doesn't know,' thought Black Sheep. Aunty Rosa had credited him in the past with petty cunning and stratagem that had never entered into his head. By the light of the sordid knowledge that she had revealed to him he paid her back full tale. In a household where the most innocent of his motives, his natural yearning for a little affection, had been interpreted into a desire for more bread and jam, or to ingratiate himself with strangers and so put Harry into the background, his work was easy. Aunty Rosa could penetrate certain kinds of hypocrisy, but not all. He set his child's wits against hers and was no more beaten. It grew monthly more and more of a trouble to read the school-books, and even the pages of the open-print story-books danced and were dim. So Black Sheep brooded in the shadows that fell about him and cut him off from the world, inventing horrible punishments for 'dear Harry,' or plotting another line of the tangled web of deception that he wrapped round Aunty Rosa.

Then the crash came and the cobwebs were broken. It was impossible to foresee everything. Aunty Rosa made personal inquiries as to Black Sheep's progress and received information that startled her. Step by step, with a delight as keen as when she convicted an underfed housemaid of the theft of cold meats, she followed the trail of Black Sheep's delinquencies. For weeks and weeks, in order to escape banishment from the book-shelves, he had made a fool of Aunty Rosa, of Harry, of God, of all the world! Horrible, most horrible, and evidence of an utterly depraved mind.

Black Sheep counted the cost. 'It will only be one big beating and then she'll put a card with "Liar" on my back, same as she did before. Harry will whack me and pray for me, and she will pray for me at prayers and tell me I'm a Child of the Devil and give me hymns to learn. But I've done all my reading and she never knew. She'll say she knew all along. She's an old liar too,' said he.

For three days Black Sheep was shut in his own bedroom—to prepare his heart. 'That means two beatings. One at school and one here. That one will hurt most.' And it fell even as he thought. He was thrashed at school before the Jews and the hubshi for the heinous crime of carrying home false reports of progress. He was thrashed at home by Aunty Rosa on the same count, and then the placard was produced. Aunty Rosa stitched it between his shoulders and bade him go for a walk with it upon him.

'If you make me do that,' said Black Sheep very quietly, 'I shall burn this house down, and perhaps I'll kill you. I don't know whether I can kill you—you're so bony—but I'll try.'

No punishment followed this blasphemy, though Black Sheep held himself ready to work his way to Aunty Rosa's withered throat, and grip there till he was beaten off. Perhaps Aunty Rosa was afraid, for Black Sheep, having reached the Nadir of Sin, bore himself with a new recklessness.

In the midst of all the trouble there came a visitor from over the seas to Downe Lodge, who knew Papa and Mamma, and was commissioned to see Punch and Judy. Black Sheep was sent to the drawing-room and charged into a solid tea-table laden with china.

'Gently, gently, little man,' said the visitor, turning Black Sheep's face to the light slowly. 'What's that big bird on the palings? '

'What bird?' asked Black Sheep.

The visitor looked deep down into Black Sheep's eyes for half a minute, and then said suddenly: 'Good God, the little chap's nearly blind! '

It was a most businesslike visitor. He gave orders, on his own responsibility, that Black Sheep was not to go to school or open a book—until Mamma came home. 'She'll be here in three weeks, as you know, of course,' said he, 'and I'm Inverarity Sahib. I ushered you into this wicked world, young man, and a nice use you seem to have made of your time. You must do nothing whatever. Can you do that?'

'Yes,' said Punch in a dazed way. He had known that Mamma was coming. There was a chance, then, of another beating. Thank Heaven, Papa wasn't coming too. Aunty Rosa had said of late that he ought to be beaten by a man.

For the next three weeks Black Sheep was strictly allowed to do nothing. He spent his time in the old nursery looking at the broken toys, for all of which account must be rendered to Mamma. Aunty Rosa hit him over the hands if even a wooden boat were broken. But that sin was of small importance compared to the other revelations, so darkly hinted at by Aunty Rosa. 'When your Mother comes, and hears what I have to tell her, she may appreciate you properly,' she said grimly, and mounted guard over Judy lest that small maiden should attempt to comfort her brother, to the peril of her soul.

And Mamma came—in a four-wheeler—fluttered with tender excitement. Such a Mamma! She was young, frivolously young, and beautiful, with delicately flushed cheeks, eyes that shone like stars, and a voice that needed no appeal of outstretched arms to draw little ones to her heart. Judy ran straight to her, but Black Sheep hesitated. Could this wonder be 'showing off'? She would not put out her arms when she knew of his crimes. Meantime was it possible that by fondling she wanted to get anything out of Black Sheep? Only all his love and all his confidence but that Black Sheep did not know. Aunty Rosa withdrew and left Mamma, kneeling between her children, half laughing, half crying, in the very hall where Punch and Judy had wept five years before.

'Well, chicks, do you remember me?'

'No,' said Judy frankly, 'but I said, "God bless Papa and Mamma" ev'vy night.'

'A little,' said Black Sheep. 'Remember I wrote to you every week, anyhow. That isn't to show off, but 'cause of what comes afterwards.'

'What comes after? What should come after, my darling boy?' And she drew him to her again. He came awkwardly, with many angles. 'Not used to petting,' said the quick Mother soul. 'The girl is.'

'She's too little to hurt any one,' thought Black Sheep, 'and if I said I'd kill her, she'd be afraid. I wonder what Aunty Rosa will tell.'

There was a constrained late dinner, at the end of which Mamma picked up Judy and put her to bed with endearments manifold. Faithless little Judy had shown her defection from Aunty Rosa already. And that lady resented it bitterly. Black Sheep rose to leave the room.

'Come and say good-night,' said Aunty Rosa, offering a withered cheek.

'Huh!' said Black Sheep. 'I never kiss you, and I'm not going to show off. Tell that woman what I've done, and see what she says.'

Black Sheep climbed into bed feeling that he had lost Heaven after a glimpse through the gates. In half an hour 'that woman' was bending over him. Black Sheep flung up his right arm. It wasn't fair to come and hit him in the dark. Even Aunty Rosa never tried that. But no blow followed.

'Are you showing off? I won't tell you anything more than Aunty Rosa has, and she doesn't know everything,' said Black Sheep as clearly as he could for the arms round his neck.

'Oh, my son—my little, little son! It was my fault—my fault, darling—and yet how could we help it? Forgive me, Punch.' The voice died out in a broken whisper, and two hot tears fell on Black Sheep's forehead.

'Has she been making you cry too?' he asked. 'You should see Jane cry. But you're nice, and Jane is a Born Liar—Aunty Rosa says so.'

'Hush, Punch, hush! My boy, don't talk like that. Try to love me a little bit—a little bit. You don't know how I want it. Punch-baba, come back to me! I am your Mother—your own Mother—and never mind the rest. I know—yes, I know, dear. It doesn't matter now. Punch, won't you care for me a little?'

It is astonishing how much petting a big boy of ten can endure when he is quite sure that there is no one to laugh at him. Black Sheep had never been made much of before, and here was this beautiful woman treating him—Black Sheep, the Child of the Devil and the inheritor of undying flame—as though he were a small God.

'I care for you a great deal, Mother dear,' he whispered at last, 'and I'm glad you've come back; but are you sure Aunty Rosa told you everything?'

'Everything. What does it matter? But—' the voice broke with a sob that was also laughter—'Punch, my poor, dear, half-blind darling, don't you think it was a little foolish of you?'

'No. It saved a lickin'.'

Mamma shuddered and slipped away in the darkness to write a long letter to Papa. Here is an extract:—

'. . . Judy is a dear, plump little prig who adores the woman, and wears with as much gravity as her religious opinions—only eight, Jack!—a venerable horse-hair atrocity which she calls her Bustle! I have just burnt it, and the child is asleep in my bed as I write. She will come to me at once. Punch I cannot quite understand. He is well nourished, but seems to have been worried into a system of small deceptions which the woman magnifies into deadly sins. Don't you recollect our own upbringing, dear, when the Fear of the Lord was so often the beginning of falsehood? I shall win Punch to me before long. I am taking the children away into the country to get them to know me, and, on the whole, I am content, or shall be when you come home, dear boy, and then, thank God, we shall be all under one roof again at last!'

Three months later, Punch, no longer Black Sheep, has discovered that he is the veritable owner of a real, live, lovely Mamma, who is also a sister, comforter, and friend, and that he must protect her till the Father comes home. Deception does not suit the part of a protector, and, when one can do anything without question, where is the use of deception?

'Mother would be awfully cross if you walked through that ditch,' says Judy, continuing a conversation.

'Mother's never angry,' says Punch. 'She'd just say, "You're a little pagal"; and that's not nice, but I'll show.'

Punch walks through the ditch and mires himself to the knees. 'Mother dear,' he shouts, 'I'm just as dirty as I can pos-sib-ly be!'

'Then change your clothes as quickly as you pos-sib-ly can!' Mother's clear voice rings out from the house. 'And don't be a little pagal!'

'There! Told you so,' says Punch. 'It's all different now, and we are just as much Mother's as if she had never gone.'

Not altogether, O Punch, for when young lips have drunk deep of the bitter waters of Hate, Suspicion, and Despair, all the Love in the world will not wholly take away that knowledge; though it may turn darkened eyes for a while to the light, and teach Faith where no Faith was.

HIS MAJESTY THE KING

'Yeth! And Chimo to sleep at ve foot of ve bed, and ve pink pikky-book, and ve bwead—'cause I will be hungwy in ve night—and vat's all, Miss Biddums. And now give me one kiss and I'll go to sleep.—So! Kite quiet. Ow! Ve pink pikky-book has slidded under ve pillow and ve bwead is cwumbling I Miss Biddums! Miss Bid-dums! I'm so uncomfy! Come and tuck me up, Miss Biddums.'

His Majesty the King was going to bed; and poor, patient Miss Biddums, who had advertised herself humbly as a 'young person, European, accustomed to the care of little children,' was forced to wait upon his royal caprices. The going to bed was always a lengthy process, because His Majesty had a convenient knack of forgetting which of his many friends, from the mehter's son to the Commissioner's daughter, he had prayed for, and, lest the Deity' should take offence, was used to, tail through his little prayers, in all reverence, five times in one evening. His Majesty the King believed in the efficacy of prayer as devoutly as he believed in Chimo the patient spaniel, or Miss Biddums, who could reach him down his gun—'wiv cursuffun caps—reel ones'—from the upper shelves of the big nursery cupboard.

At the door of the nursery his authority stopped. Beyond lay the empire of his father and mother—two very terrible people who had no time to waste upon His Majesty the King. His voice was lowered when he passed the frontier of his own dominions, his actions were fettered, and his soul was filled with awe because of the grim man who lived among a wilderness of pigeon-holes and the most fascinating pieces of red tape, and the wonderful woman who was always getting into or stepping out of the big carriage.

To the one belonged the mysteries of the 'duftar-room,' to the other the great, reflected wilderness of the 'Memsahib's room,' where the shiny, scented dresses hung on pegs, miles and miles up in the air, and the just-seen plateau of the toilet-table revealed an acreage of speckly combs, broidered 'hanafitch-bags,' and 'white-headed' brushes.

There was no room for His Majesty the King either in official reserve or worldly gorgeousness. He had discovered that, ages and ages ago—before even Chimo came to the house, or Miss Biddums had ceased grizzling over a packet of greasy letters which appeared to be her chief treasure on earth. His

Majesty the King, therefore, wisely confined himself to his own territories, where only Miss Biddums, and she feebly, disputed his sway.

From Miss Biddums he had picked up his simple theology and welded it to the legends of Gods and Devils that he had learned in the servants' quarters.

To Miss Biddums he confided with equal trust his tattered garments and his more serious griefs. She would make everything whole. She knew exactly how the Earth had been born, and had reassured the trembling soul of His Majesty the King that terrible time in July when it rained continuously for seven days and seven nights, and—there was no Ark ready and all the ravens had flown away! She was the most powerful person with whom he was brought into contact—always excepting the two remote and silent people beyond the nursery door.

How was His Majesty the King to know that, six years ago, in the summer of his birth, Mrs. Austell, turning over her husband's papers, had come upon the intemperate letter of a foolish woman who had been carried away by the silent man's strength and personal beauty? How could he tell what evil the overlooked slip of notepaper had wrought in the mind of a desperately jealous wife? How could he, despite his wisdom, guess that his mother had chosen to make of it excuse for a bar and a division between herself and her husband, that strengthened and grew harder to break with each year; that she, having unearthed this skeleton in the cupboard, had trained it into a household God which should be about their path and about their bed, and poison all their ways?

These things were beyond the province of His Majesty the King. He only knew that his father was daily absorbed in some mysterious work for a thing called the Sirkar, and that his mother was the victim alternately of the Nautch and the Burra-khana. To these entertainments she was escorted by a Captain-Man for whom His Majesty the King had no regard.

'He doesn't laugh,' he argued with Miss Biddums, who would fain have taught him charity. 'He only makes faces wiv his mouf, and when he wants to o-muse me I am not o-mused.' And His Majesty the King shook his head as one who knew the deceitfulness of this world.

Morning and evening it was his duty to salute his father and mother—the former with a grave shake of the hand, and the latter with an equally grave kiss. Once, indeed, he had put his arms round his mother's neck, in the fashion he used towards Miss Biddums. The openwork of his sleeve-edge caught in an ear-ring, and the last stage of His Majesty's little overture was a suppressed scream and summary dismissal to the nursery.

'It is w'ong,' thought His Majesty the King, 'to hug Memsahibs wiv fings in veir ears. I will amember.' He never repeated the experiment.

Miss Biddums, it must be confessed, spoilt him as much as his nature admitted, in some sort of recompense for what she called 'the hard ways of his Papa and Mamma.' She, like her charge, knew nothing of the trouble between man and wife—the savage contempt for a woman's stupidity on the one side, or the dull, rankling anger on the other. Miss Biddums had looked after many little children in her time, and served in many establishments. Being a discreet woman, she observed little and said less, and, when her pupils went over the sea to the Great Unknown, which she, with touching confidence in her hearers, called 'Home,' packed up her slender belongings and sought for employment afresh, lavishing all her love on each successive batch of ingrates. Only His Majesty the King had repaid her affection with interest; and in his uncomprehending ears she had told the tale of nearly all her hopes, her aspirations, the hopes that were dead, and the dazzling glories of her ancestral home in 'Calcutta, close to Wellington Square.'

Everything above the average was in the eyes of His Majesty the King 'Calcutta good.' When Miss Biddums had crossed his royal will, he reversed the epithet to vex that estimable lady, and all things evil were, until the tears of repentance swept away spite, 'Calcutta bad.'

Now and again Miss Biddums begged for him the rare pleasure of a day in the society of 'the Commissioner's child—the wilful four-year-old Patsie, who, to the intense amazement of His Majesty the King, was idolised by her parents. On thinking the question out at length, by roads unknown to those who have left childhood behind, he came to the conclusion that Patsie was petted because she wore a big blue sash and yellow hair.

This precious discovery he kept to himself. The yellow hair was absolutely beyond his power, his own tousled wig being potato-brown; but something might be done towards the blue sash. He tied a large knot in his mosquito-curtains in order to remember to consult Patsie on their next meeting. She was the only child he had ever spoken to, and almost the only one that he had ever seen. The little memory and the very large and ragged knot held good.

'Patsie, lend me your blue wiban,' said His Majesty the King.

'You'll buwy it,' said Patsie doubtfully, mindful of certain atrocities committed on her doll.

'No, I won't—two of an honour. It's for me to wear.'

'Pooh!' said Patsie. 'Boys don't wear sa-ashes. Zey's only for dirls.'

'I didn't know.' The face of His Majesty the King fell.

'Who wants ribands? Are you playing horses, chickabiddies?' said the Commissioner's wife, stepping into the veranda.

'Toby wanted my sash,' explained Patsie.

'I don't now,' said His Majesty the King hastily, feeling that with one of these terrible 'grown-ups' his poor little secret would be shamelessly wrenched from him, and perhaps—most burning desecration of all—laughed at.

'I'll give you a cracker-cap,' said the Commissioner's wife. 'Come along with me, Toby, and we'll choose it.'

The cracker-cap was a stiff, three-pointed vermilion-and-tinsel splendour. His Majesty the King fitted it on his royal brow. The Commissioner's wife had a face that children instinctively trusted, and her action, as she adjusted the toppling middle spike, was tender.

'Will it do as well?' stammered His Majesty the King.

'As what, little one?'

'As ve wiban?'

'Oh, quite. Go and look at yourself in the glass.'

The words were spoken in all sincerity, and to help forward any absurd 'dressing-up' amusement that the children might take into their minds. But the young savage has a keen sense of the ludicrous. His Majesty the King swung the great cheval-glass down, and saw his head crowned with the staring horror of a fool's cap—a thing which his father would rend to pieces if it ever came into his office. He plucked it off, and burst into tears.

'Toby,' said the Commissioner's wife gravely, 'you shouldn't give way to temper. I am very sorry to see it. It's wrong.'

His Majesty the King sobbed inconsolably, and the heart of Patsie's mother was touched. She drew the child on to her knee. Clearly it was not temper alone.

'What is it, Toby? Won't you tell me? Aren't you Well? '

The torrent of sobs and speech met, and fought for a time, with chokings and gulpings and gasps. Then, in a sudden rush, His Majesty the King was delivered of a few inarticulate sounds, followed by the words: 'Go a—way, you—dirty—little Debbil!'

'Toby! What do you mean?'

'It's what he'd say. I know it is! He said vat when vere was only a little, little eggy mess, on my t-t-unic; and he'd say it again, and laugh, if I went in wiv vat on my head.'

'Who would say that?'

'M-m-my Papa! And I fought if I had ve blue wiban, he'd let me play in ve waste-paper basket under ve table.'

'What blue riband, childie?'

'Ve same vat Patsie had—ve big blue wiban w-w-wound my t-t-tummy!'

'What is it, Toby? There's something on your mind. Tell me all about it, and perhaps I can help.'

''Isn't anyfing,' sniffed His Majesty, mindful of his manhood, and raising his head from the motherly bosom upon which it was resting. 'I only fought vat you—you petted Patsie 'cause she had ve blue wiban, and—and if I'd had ve blue wiban too, m-my Papa w-would pet me.'

The secret was out, and His Majesty the King sobbed bitterly in spite of the arms around him and the murmur of comfort on his heated little forehead.

Enter Patsie tumultuously, embarrassed by several lengths of the Commissioner's pet mahseer-rod. 'Tum along, Toby! Zere's a chu-chu lizard in ze chick, and I've told Chimo to watch him till we tum. If we poke him wiz zis his tail will go wiggle-wiggle and fall off. Tum along! I can't weach.'

'I'm comin',' said His Majesty the King, climbing down from the Commissioner's wife's knee after a hasty kiss.

Two minutes later, the chu-chu lizard's tail was wriggling on the matting of the veranda, and the children were gravely poking it with splinters from the chick, to urge its exhausted vitality into 'just one wiggle more, 'cause it doesn't hurt chu-chu.'

The Commissioner's wife stood in the doorway and watched. 'Poor little mite! A blue sash—and my own precious Patsie! I wonder if the best of us, or we who love them best, ever understand what goes on in their topsy-turvy little heads.'

She went indoors to devise a tea for His Majesty the King.

'Their souls aren't in their tummies at that age in this climate,' said the Commissioner's wife, 'but they are not far off. I wonder if I could make Mrs. Austell understand. Poor little chap!'

With simple craft, the Commissioner's wife called on Mrs. Austell and spoke long and lovingly about children; inquiring specially for His Majesty the King.

'He's with his governess,' said Mrs. Austell, and the tone showed that she was not interested.

The Commissioner's wife, unskilled in the art of war, continued her questionings. 'I don't know,' said Mrs. Austell. 'These things are left to Miss Biddums, and, of course, she does not ill-treat the child.'

The Commissioner's wife left hastily. The last sentence jarred upon her nerves. 'Doesn't ill-treat the child! As if that were all! I wonder what Tom would say if I only "didn't ill-treat" Patsie! '

Thenceforward, His Majesty the King was an honoured guest at the Commissioner's house, and the chosen friend of Patsie, with whom he blundered into as many scrapes as the compound and the servants' quarters afforded. Patsie's Mamma was always ready to give counsel, help, and sympathy, and, if need were and callers few, to enter into their games with an abandon that would have shocked the sleek-haired subalterns who squirmed painfully in their chairs when they came to call on her whom they profanely nicknamed 'Mother Bunch.'

Yet, in spite of Patsie and Patsie's Mamma, and the love that these two lavished upon him, His Majesty the King fell grievously from grace, and committed no less a sin than that of theft—unknown, it is true, but burdensome.

There came a man to the door one day, when His Majesty was playing in the hall and the bearer had gone to dinner, with a packet for His Majesty's Mamma. And he put it upon the hall-table, and said that there was no answer, and departed.

Presently, the pattern of the dado ceased to interest His Majesty, while the packet, a white, neatly-wrapped one of fascinating shape, interested him very much indeed. His Mamma was out, so was Miss

Biddums, and there was pink string round the packet. He greatly desired pink string. It would help him in many of his little businesses—the haulage across the floor of his small cane-chair, the torturing of Chimo, who could never understand harness—and so forth. If he took the string it would be his own, and nobody would be any the wiser. He certainly could not pluck up sufficient courage to ask Mamma for it. Wherefore, mounting upon a chair, he carefully untied the string and, behold, the stiff white paper spread out in four directions, and revealed a beautiful little leather box with gold lines upon it! He tried to replace the string, but that was a failure. So he opened the box to get full satisfaction for his iniquity, and saw a most beautiful Star that shone and winked, and was altogether lovely and desirable.

'Vat,' said His Majesty meditatively, 'is a 'parkle cwown, like what I will wear when I go to Heaven. I will wear it on my head—Miss Biddums says so. I would like to wear it now. I would like to play wiv it. I will take it away and play wiv it, vewy careful, until Mamma asks for it. I fink it was bought for me to play wiv—same as my cart.'

His Majesty the King was arguing against his conscience, and he knew it, for he thought immediately after: 'Never mind, I will keep it to play wiv until Mamma says where is it, and then I will say—"I tookt it and I am sorry." I will not hurt it because it is a 'parkle cwown. But Miss Biddums will tell me to put it back. I will not show it to Miss Biddums.'

If Mamma had come in at that moment all would have gone well. She did not, and His Majesty the King stuffed paper, case, and jewel into the breast of his blouse and marched to the nursery.

'When Mamma asks I will tell,' was the salve that he laid upon his conscience. But Mamma never asked, and for three whole days His Majesty the King gloated over his treasure. It was of no earthly use to him, but it was splendid, and, for aught he knew, something dropped from the heavens themselves. Still Mamma made no inquiries, and it seemed to him, in his furtive peeps, as though the shiny stones grew dim. What was the use of a ''parkle cwown' if it made a little boy feel all bad in his inside? He had the pink string as well as the other treasure, but greatly he wished that he had not gone beyond the string. It was his first experience of iniquity, and it pained him after the flush of possession and secret delight in the ''parkle cwown' had died away.

Each day that he delayed rendered confession to the people beyond the nursery doors more impossible. Now and again he determined to put himself in the path of the beautifully-attired lady as she was going out, and explain that he and no one else was the possessor of a ''parkle cwown,' most beautiful and quite uninquired-for. But she passed hurriedly to her carriage, and the opportunity was gone before His Majesty the King could draw the deep breath which clinches noble resolve. The dread secret cut him off from Miss Biddums, Patsie, and the Commissioner's wife, and—doubly hard fate—when he brooded over it Patsie said, and told her mother, that he was cross.

The days were very long to His Majesty the King, and the nights longer still. Miss Biddums had informed him, more than once, what was the ultimate destiny of 'fieves,' and when he passed the interminable mud flanks of the Central jail, he shook in his little strapped shoes.

But release came after an afternoon spent in playing boats by the edge of the tank at the bottom of the garden. His Majesty the King went to tea, and, for the first time in his memory, the meal revolted him. His nose was very cold, and his cheeks were burning hot. There was a weight about his feet, and he pressed his head several times to make sure that it was not swelling as he sat.

'I feel vewy funny,' said His Majesty the King, rubbing his nose. 'Vere's a buzz-buzz in my head.'

He went to bed quietly. Miss Biddums was out and the bearer undressed him.

The sin of the ''parkle cwown' was forgotten in the acuteness of the discomfort to which he roused after a leaden sleep of some hours. He was thirsty, and the bearer had forgotten to leave the drinking-water. 'Miss Biddums! Miss Biddums! I'm so kirsty!'

No answer. Miss Biddums had leave to attend the wedding of a Calcutta schoolmate. His Majesty the King had forgotten that.

'I want a dwink of water,' he cried, but his voice was dried up in his throat. 'I want a dwink! Vere is ve glass?'

He sat up in bed and looked round. There was a murmur of voices from the other side of the nursery door. It was better to face the terrible unknown than to choke in the dark. He slipped out of bed, but his feet were strangely wilful, and he reeled once or twice. Then he pushed the door open and staggered—a puffed and purple-faced little figure—into the brilliant light of the dining-room full of pretty ladies.

'I'm vewy hot! I'm vewy uncomfitivle,' moaned His Majesty the King, clinging to the portiere, 'and vere's no water in ve glass, and I'm so kirsty. Give me a dwink of water.'

An apparition in black and white—His Majesty the King could hardly see distinctly—lifted him up to the level of the table, and felt his wrists and forehead. The water came, and he drank deeply, his teeth chattering against the edge of the tumbler. Then every one seemed to go away—every one except the huge man in black and white, who carried him back to his bed; the mother and father following. And the sin of the ''parkle cwown' rushed back and took possession of the terrified soul.

'I'm a fief!' he gasped. 'I want to tell Miss Biddums vat I'm a fief. Vere is Miss Biddums?'

Miss Biddums had come and was bending over him. 'I'm a fief,' he whispered. 'A fief—like ve men in ve pwison. But I'll tell now. I tookt—I tookt ve 'parkle cwown when ve man vat came left it in ve hall. I bwoke ve paper and ve little bwown box, and it looked shiny, and I tookt it to play wiv, and I was afwaid. It's in ve dooly box at ve bottom. No one never asked for it, but I was afwaid. Oh, go an' get ve dooly-box!'

Miss Biddums obediently stooped to the lowest shelf of the almirah and unearthed the big paper box in which His Majesty the King kept his dearest possessions. Under the tin soldiers, and a layer of mud pellets for a pellet-bow, winked and blazed a diamond star, wrapped roughly in a half-sheet of notepaper whereon were a few words.

Somebody was crying at the head of the bed, and a man's hand touched the forehead of His Majesty the King, who grasped the packet and spread it on the bed.

'Vat is ve 'parkle cwown,' he said, and wept bitterly; for now that he had made restitution he would fain have kept the shining splendour with him.

'It concerns you too,' said a voice at the head of the bed. 'Read the note. This is not the time to keep back anything.'

The note was curt, very much to the point, and signed by a single initial. 'If you wear this tomorrow night I shall know what to expect.' The date was three weeks old.

A whisper followed, and the deeper voice returned: 'And you drifted as far apart as that! I think it makes us quits now, doesn't it? Oh, can't we drop this folly once and for all? Is it worth it, darling?'

'Kiss me too,' said His Majesty the King dreamily. 'You isn't vewy angwy, is you?'

The fever burned itself out, and His Majesty the King slept.

When he waked, it was in a new world—peopled by his father and mother as well as Miss Biddums; and there was much love in that world and no morsel of fear, and more petting than was good for several little boys. His Majesty the King was too young to moralise on the uncertainty of things human, or he would have been impressed with the singular advantages of crime—ay, black sin. Behold, he had stolen the "parkle cwown,' and his reward was Love, and the right to play in the waste-paper basket under the table 'for always.'

He trotted over to spend an afternoon with Patsie, and the Commissioner's wife would have kissed him. 'No, not vere,' said His Majesty the King, with superb insolence, fencing one corner of his mouth with his hand. 'Vat's my Mamma's place—vere she kisses me.'

'Oh!' said the Commissioner's wife briefly. Then to herself: 'Well, I suppose I ought to be glad for his sake. Children are selfish little grubs and—I've got my Patsie.'

THE DRUMS OF THE FORE AND AFT

In the Army List they still stand as "The Fore and Fit Princess Hohenzollern-Sigmaringen-Anspach's Merther-Tydfilshire Own Royal Loyal Light Infantry, Regimental District 329A," but the Army through all its barracks and canteens knows them now as the "Fore and Aft." They may in time do something that shall make their new title honourable, but at present they are bitterly ashamed, and the man who calls them "Fore and Aft" does so at the risk of the head which is on his shoulders.

Two words breathed into the stables of a certain Cavalry Regiment will bring the men out into the streets with belts and mops and bad language; but a whisper of "Fore and Aft" will bring out this regiment with rifles.

Their one excuse is that they came again and did their best to finish the job in style. But for a time all their world knows that they were openly beaten, whipped, dumb-cowed, shaking and afraid. The men know it; their officers know it; the Horse Guards know it, and when the next war comes the enemy will know it also. There are two or three regiments of the Line that have a black mark against their names which they will then wipe out; and it will be excessively inconvenient for the troops upon whom they do their wiping.

The courage of the British soldier is officially supposed to be above proof, and, as a general rule, it is so. The exceptions are decently shovelled out of sight, only to be referred to in the freshest of unguarded talk that occasionally swamps a Mess-table at midnight. Then one hears strange and horrible stories of men not following their officers, of orders being given by those who had no right to give them, and of disgrace that, but for the standing luck of the British Army, might have ended in brilliant disaster. These are unpleasant stories to listen to, and the Messes tell them under their breath, sitting by the big wood fires, and the young officer bows his head and thinks to himself, please God, his men shall never behave unhandily.

The British soldier is not altogether to be blamed for occasional lapses; but this verdict he should not know. A moderately intelligent General will waste six months in mastering the craft of the particular war that he may be waging; a Colonel may utterly misunderstand the capacity of his regiment for three months after it has taken the field, and even a Company Commander may err and be deceived as to the temper and temperament of his own handful: wherefore the soldier, and the soldier of to-day more particularly, should not be blamed for falling back. He should be shot or hanged afterwards—to encourage the others; but he should not be vilified in newspapers, for that is want of tact and waste of space.

He has, let us say, been in the service of the Empress for, perhaps, four years. He will leave in another two years. He has no inherited morals, and four years are not sufficient to drive toughness into his fibre, or to teach him how holy a thing is his Regiment. He wants to drink, he wants to enjoy himself—in India he wants to save money—and he does not in the least like getting hurt. He has received just sufficient education to make him understand half the purport of the orders he receives, and to speculate on the nature of clean, incised, and shattering wounds. Thus, if he is told to deploy under fire preparatory to an attack, he knows that he runs a very great risk of being killed while he is deploying, and suspects that he is being thrown away to gain ten minutes' time. He may either deploy with desperate swiftness, or he may shuffle, or bunch, or break, according to the discipline under which he has lain for four years.

Armed with imperfect knowledge, cursed with the rudiments of an imagination, hampered by the intense selfishness of the lower classes, and unsupported by any regimental associations, this young man is suddenly introduced to an enemy who in eastern lands is always ugly, generally tall and hairy, and frequently noisy. If he looks to the right and the left and sees old soldiers—men of twelve years' service, who, he knows, know what they are about—taking a charge, rush, or demonstration without embarrassment, he is consoled and applies his shoulder to the butt of his rifle with a stout heart. His peace is the greater if he hears a senior, who has taught him his soldiering and broken his head on occasion, whispering: "They'll shout and carry on like this for five minutes. Then they'll rush in, and then we've got 'em by the short hairs!"

But, on the other hand, if he sees only men of his own term of service, turning white and playing with their triggers and saying: "What the Hell's up now?" while the Company Commanders are sweating into their sword-hilts and shouting: "Front rank, fix bayonets. Steady there—steady! Sight for three hundred—no, for five! Lie down, all! Steady! Front rank kneel!" and so forth, he becomes unhappy, and grows acutely miserable when he hears a comrade turn over with the rattle of fire-irons falling into the fender, and the grunt of a pole-axed ox. If he can be moved about a little and allowed to watch the effect of his own fire on the enemy he feels merrier, and may be then worked up to the blind passion of fighting, which is, contrary to general belief, controlled by a chilly Devil and shakes men like ague. If he is not moved about, and begins to feel cold at the pit of the stomach, and in that crisis is badly mauled and hears orders that were never given, he will break, and he will break badly, and of all things under the light of the Sun there is nothing more terrible than a broken British regiment. When the worst comes to the worst and the panic is really epidemic, the men must be e'en let go, and the Company Commanders had better escape to the enemy and stay there for safety's sake. If they can be made to come again they are not pleasant men to meet; because they will not break twice.

About thirty years from this date, when we have succeeded in half-educating everything that wears trousers, our Army will be a beautifully unreliable machine. It will know too much and it will do too little. Later still, when all men are at the mental level of the officer of to-day, it will sweep the earth. Speaking roughly, you must employ either blackguards or gentlemen, or, best of all, blackguards commanded by gentlemen, to do butcher's work with efficiency and despatch. The ideal soldier should, of course, think for himself—the "Pocket-book" says so. Unfortunately, to attain this virtue, he has to pass through the phase of thinking of himself, and that is misdirected genius. A blackguard may be slow to think for himself, but he is genuinely anxious to kill, and a little punishment teaches him how to guard his own skin and perforate another's. A powerfully prayerful Highland Regiment, officered by rank Presbyterians, is, perhaps, one degree more terrible in action than a hard-bitten thousand of irresponsible Irish ruffians led by most improper young unbelievers. But these things prove the rule—which is that the midway men are not to be trusted alone. They have ideas about the value of life and an upbringing that has not taught them to go on and take the chances. They are carefully unprovided with a backing of comrades who have been shot over, and until that backing is re-introduced, as a great many Regimental Commanders intend it shall be, they are more liable to disgrace themselves than the size of the Empire or the dignity of the Army allows. Their officers are as good as good can be, because their training begins early, and God has arranged that a clean-run youth of the British middle classes shall, in the matter of backbone, brains, and bowels, surpass all other youths. For this reason a child of eighteen will stand up, doing nothing, with a tin sword in his hand and joy in his heart until he is dropped. If he dies, he dies like a gentleman. If he lives, he writes Home that he has been "potted," "sniped," "chipped," or "cut over," and sits down to besiege Government for a wound-gratuity until the next little war breaks out, when he perjures himself before a Medical Board, blarneys his Colonel, burns incense round his Adjutant, and is allowed to go to the Front once more.

Which homily brings me directly to a brace of the most finished little fiends that ever banged drum or tootled fife in the Band of a British Regiment. They ended their sinful career by open and flagrant mutiny and were shot for it. Their names were Jakin and Lew—Piggy Lew—and they were bold, bad drummer-boys, both of them frequently birched by the Drum-Major of the Fore and Aft.—Jakin was a stunted child of fourteen, and Lew was about the same age. When not looked after, they smoked and drank. They swore habitually after the manner of the Barrack-room, which is cold swearing and comes from between clenched teeth, and they fought religiously once a week. Jakin had sprung from some London gutter, and may or may not have passed through Dr. Barnardo's hands ere he arrived at the dignity of drummer-boy. Lew could remember nothing except the Regiment and the delight of listening to the Band from his earliest years. He hid somewhere in his grimy little soul a genuine love for music, and was most mistakenly furnished with the head of a cherub: insomuch that beautiful ladies who watched the Regiment in church were wont to speak of him as a "darling." They never heard his vitriolic comments on their manners and morals, as he walked back to barracks with the Band and matured fresh causes of offence against Jakin.

The other drummer-boys hated both lads on account of their illogical conduct. Jakin might be pounding Lew, or Lew might be rubbing Jakin's head in the dirt, but any attempt at aggression on the part of an outsider was met by the combined forces of Lew and Jakin; and the consequences were painful. The boys were the Ishmaels of the corps, but wealthy Ishmaels, for they sold battles in alternate weeks for the sport of the barracks when they were not pitted against other boys; and thus amassed money.

On this particular day there was dissension in the camp. They had just been convicted afresh of smoking, which is bad for little boys who use plug-tobacco, and Lew's contention was that Jakin had "stunk so 'orrid bad from keepin' the pipe in pocket," that he and he alone was responsible for the birching they were both tingling under.

"I tell you I 'id the pipe back o' barracks," said Jakin pacifically.

"You're a bloomin' liar," said Lew without heat.

"You're a bloomin' little barstard," said Jakin, strong in the knowledge that his own ancestry was unknown.

Now there is one word in the extended vocabulary of barrack-room abuse that cannot pass without comment. You may call a man a thief and risk nothing. You may even call him a coward without finding more than a boot whiz past your ear, but you must not call a man a bastard unless you are prepared to prove it on his front teeth.

"You might ha' kep' that till I wasn't so sore," said Lew sorrowfully, dodging round Jakin's guard.

"I'll make you sorer," said Jakin genially, and got home on Lew's alabaster forehead. All would have gone well and this story, as the books say, would never have been written, had not his evil fate prompted the Bazar-Sergeant's son, a long, employless man of five-and-twenty, to put in an appearance after the first round. He was eternally in need of money, and knew that the boys had silver.

"Fighting again," said he. "I'll report you to my father, and he'll report you to the Colour-Sergeant."

"What's that to you?" said Jakin with an unpleasant dilation of the nostrils.

"Oh! nothing to me. You'll get into trouble, and you've been up too often to afford that."

"What the Hell do you know about what we've done?" asked Lew the Seraph. "You aren't in the Army, you lousy, cadging civilian."

He closed in on the man's left flank.

"Jes' 'cause you find two gentlemen settlin' their diff'rences with their fistes you stick in your ugly nose where you aren't wanted. Run 'ome to your 'arf-caste slut of a Ma—or we'll give you what-for," said Jakin.

The man attempted reprisals by knocking the boys' heads together. The scheme would have succeeded had not Jakin punched him vehemently in the stomach, or had Lew refrained from kicking his shins. They fought together, bleeding and breathless, for half an hour, and, after heavy punishment, triumphantly pulled down their opponent as terriers pull down a jackal.

"Now," gasped Jakin, "I'll give you what-for." He proceeded to pound the man's features while Lew stamped on the outlying portions of his anatomy. Chivalry is not a strong point in the composition of the average drummer-boy. He fights, as do his betters, to make his mark.

Ghastly was the ruin that escaped, and awful was the wrath of the Bazar-Sergeant. Awful too was the scene in Orderly-room when the two reprobates appeared to answer the charge of half-murdering a "civilian." The Bazar-Sergeant thirsted for a criminal action, and his son lied. The boys stood to attention while the black clouds of evidence accumulated.

"You little devils are more trouble than the rest of the Regiment put together," said the Colonel angrily. "One might as well admonish thistledown, and I can't well put you in cells or under stoppages. You must be birched again."

"Beg y' pardon, Sir. Can't we say nothin' in our own defence, Sir?" shrilled Jakin.

"Hey! What? Are you going to argue with me?" said the Colonel.

"No, Sir," said Lew. "But if a man come to you, Sir, and said he was going to report you, Sir, for 'aving a bit of a turn-up with a friend, Sir, an' wanted to get money out o' you, Sir—"

The Orderly-room exploded in a roar of laughter. "Well?" said the Colonel.

"That was what that measly jarnwar there did, Sir, and 'e'd 'a' done it, Sir, if we 'adn't prevented 'im. We didn't 'it 'im much, Sir. 'E 'adn't no manner o' right to interfere with us, Sir. I don't mind bein' birched by the Drum-Major, Sir, nor yet reported by any Corp'ral, but I'm—but I don't think it's fair, Sir, for a civilian to come an' talk over a man in the Army."

A second shout of laughter shook the Orderly-room, but the Colonel was grave.

"What sort of characters have these boys?" he asked of the Regimental Sergeant-Major.

"Accordin' to the Bandmaster, Sir," returned that revered official—the only soul in the Regiment whom the boys feared—"they do everything but lie, Sir."

"Is it like we'd go for that man for fun, Sir?" said Lew, pointing to the plaintiff.

"Oh, admonished—admonished!" said the Colonel testily, and when the boys had gone he read the Bazar-Sergeant's son a lecture on the sin of unprofitable meddling, and gave orders that the Bandmaster should keep the Drums in better discipline.

"If either of you come to practice again with so much as a scratch on your two ugly little faces," thundered the Bandmaster, "I'll tell the Drum-Major to take the skin off your backs. Understand that, you young devils."

Then he repented of his speech for just the length of time that Lew, looking like a seraph in red worsted embellishments, took the place of one of the trumpets—in hospital—and rendered the echo of a battle-piece. Lew certainly was a musician, and had often in his more exalted moments expressed a yearning to master every instrument of the Band.

"There's nothing to prevent your becoming a Bandmaster, Lew," said the Bandmaster, who had composed waltzes of his own, and worked day and night in the interests of the Band.

"What did he say?" demanded Jakin after practice.

"Said I might be a bloomin' Bandmaster, an' be asked in to 'ave a glass o' sherry wine on Mess-nights."

"Ho! Said you might be a bloomin' noncombatant, did 'e! That's just about wot 'e would say. When I've put in my boy's service—it's a bloomin' shame that doesn't count for pension—I'll take on as a privit. Then I'll be a Lance in a year—knowin' what I know about the ins an' outs o' things. In three years I'll be a bloomin' Sergeant. I won't marry then, not I! I'll 'old on and learn the orf'cers' ways an' apply for exchange into a reg'ment that doesn't know all about me. Then I'll be a bloomin' orf'cer. Then I'll ask you to 'ave a glass o' sherry wine, Mister Lew, an' you'll bloomin' well 'ave to stay in the hanty-room while the Mess-Sergeant brings it to your dirty 'ands."—

"S'pose I'm going to be a Bandmaster? Not I, quite. I'll be a orf'cer too. There's nothin' like takin' to a thing an' stickin' to it, the Schoolmaster says. The Reg'ment don't go 'ome for another seven years. I'll be a Lance then or near to."

Thus the boys discussed their futures, and conducted themselves piously for a week. That is to say, Lew started a flirtation with the Colour-Sergeant's daughter, aged thirteen—"not," as he explained to Jakin, "with any intention o' matrimony, but by way o' keep in' my 'and in." And the black-haired Cris Delighan enjoyed that flirtation more than previous ones, and the other drummer-boys raged furiously together, and Jakin preached sermons on the dangers of bein' tangled along o' petticoats."

But neither love nor virtue would have held Lew long in the paths of propriety had not the rumour gone abroad that the Regiment was to be sent on active service, to take part in a war which, for the sake of brevity, we will call "The War of the Lost Tribes."

The barracks had the rumour almost before the Mess-room, and of all the nine hundred men in barracks, not ten had seen a shot fired in anger. The Colonel had, twenty years ago, assisted at a Frontier expedition; one of the Majors had seen service at the Cape; a confirmed deserter in E Company had helped to clear streets in Ireland; but that was all. The Regiment had been put by for many years. The overwhelming mass of its rank and file had from three to four years' service; the non-commissioned officers were under thirty years old; and men and sergeants alike had forgotten to speak of the stories written in brief upon the Colours—the New Colours that had been formally blessed by an Archbishop in England ere the Regiment came away.

They wanted to go to the Front—they were enthusiastically anxious to go—but they had no knowledge of what war meant, and there was none to tell them. They were an educated regiment, the percentage of school-certificates in their ranks was high, and most of the men could do more than read and write. They had been recruited in loyal observance of the territorial idea; but they themselves had no notion of that idea. They were made up of drafts from an over-populated manufacturing district. The system had put flesh and muscle upon their small bones, but it could not put heart into the sons of those who for generations had done overmuch work for overscanty pay, had sweated in drying-rooms, stooped over looms, coughed among white-lead, and shivered on lime-barges. The men had found food and rest in the Army, and now they were going to fight "niggers"—people who ran away if you shook a stick at them. Wherefore they cheered lustily when the rumour ran, and the shrewd, clerkly non-commissioned officers speculated on the chances of batta and of saving their pay. At Headquarters men said: "The Fore and Fit have never been under fire within the last generation. Let us, therefore, break them in easily by setting them to guard lines of communication." And this would have been done but for the fact that British Regiments were wanted—badly wanted—at the Front, and there were doubtful Native Regiments that could fill the minor duties. "Brigade 'em with two strong Regiments," said Headquarters. "They may be knocked about a bit, but they'll learn their business before they come through. Nothing like a night-alarm and a little cutting-up of stragglers to make a Regiment smart in the field. Wait till they've had half a dozen sentries' throats cut."

The Colonel wrote with delight that the temper of his men was excellent, that the Regiment was all that could be wished, and as sound as a bell. The Majors smiled with a sober joy, and the subalterns waltzed in pairs down the Mess-room after dinner, and nearly shot themselves at revolver-practice. But there was consternation in the hearts of Jakin and Lew. What was to be done with the Drums? Would the Band go to the Front? How many of the Drums would accompany the Regiment?

They took counsel together, sitting in a tree and smoking.

"It's more than a bloomin' toss-up they'll leave us be'ind at the Depôt with the women. You'll like that," said Jakin sarcastically.

"Cause o' Cris, y' mean? Wot's a woman, or a 'ole bloomin' Depôt o' women, 'longside o' the chanst of field-service? You know I'm as keen on goin' as you," said Lew.

"Wish I was a bloomin' bugler," said Jakin sadly. "They'll take Tom Kidd along, that I can plaster a wall with, an' like as not they won't take us."

"Then let's go an' make Tom Kidd so bloomin' sick 'e can't bugle no more. You 'old 'is 'ands an' I'll kick him," said Lew, wriggling on the branch.

"That ain't no good neither. We ain't the sort o' characters to presoom on our rep'tations—they're bad. If they have the Band at the Depôt we don't go, and no error there. If they take the Band we may get cast for medical unfitness. Are you medical fit, Piggy?" said Jakin, digging Lew in the ribs with force.

"Yus," said Lew with an oath. "The Doctor says your 'eart's weak through smokin' on an empty stummick. Throw a chest an' I'll try yer."

Jakin threw out his chest, which Lew smote with all his might. Jakin turned very pale, gasped, crowed, screwed up his eyes, and said—"That's all right."

"You'll do," said Lew. "I've 'eard o' men dying when you 'it 'em fair on the breastbone."

"Don't bring us no nearer goin', though," said Jakin. "Do you know where we're ordered?"

"Gawd knows, an' 'E won't split on a pal. Somewheres up to the Front to kill Paythans—hairy big beggars that turn you inside out if they get 'old o' you. They say their women are good-looking, too."

"Any loot?" asked the abandoned Jakin.

"Not a bloomin' anna, they say, unless you dig up the ground an' see what the niggers 'ave 'id. They're a poor lot." Jakin stood upright on the branch and gazed across the plain.

"Lew," said he, "there's the Colonel coming. 'Colonel's a good old beggar. Let's go an' talk to 'im."

Lew nearly fell out of the tree at the audacity of the suggestion. Like Jakin he feared not God, neither regarded he Man, but there are limits even to the audacity of a drummer-boy, and to speak to a Colonel was—

But Jakin had slid down the trunk and doubled in the direction of the Colonel. That officer was walking wrapped in thought and visions of a C.B.—yes, even a K.C.B., for had he not at command one of the best Regiments of the Line—the Fore and Fit? And he was aware of two small boys charging down upon him. Once before it had been solemnly reported to him that "the Drums were in a state of mutiny," Jakin and Lew being the ringleaders. This looked like an organised conspiracy. The boys halted at twenty yards, walked to the regulation four paces, and saluted together, each as well set-up as a ramrod and little taller.

The Colonel was in a genial mood; the boys appeared very forlorn and unprotected on the desolate plain, and one of them was handsome.

"Well!" said the Colonel, recognising them. "Are you going to pull me down in the open? I'm sure I never interfere with you, even though"—he sniffed suspiciously—"you have been smoking."

It was time to strike while the iron was hot. Their hearts beat tumultuously.

"Beg y' pardon, Sir," began Jakin. "The Reg'ment's ordered on active service, Sir?"

"So I believe," said the Colonel courteously.

"Is the Band goin', Sir?" said both together. Then, without pause, "We're goin', Sir, ain't we?"

"You!" said the Colonel, stepping back the more fully to take in the two small figures. "You! You'd die in the first march."

"No, we wouldn't, Sir. We can march with the Reg'ment anywheres—p'rade an' anywhere else," said Jakin.

"If Tom Kidd goes 'e'll shut up like a clasp-knife," said Lew. "Tom 'as very-close veins in both 'is legs, Sir."

"Very how much?"

"Very-close veins, Sir. That's why they swells after long p'rade, Sir. If 'e can go, we can go, Sir."

Again the Colonel looked at them long and intently.

"Yes, the Band is going," he said as gravely as though he had been addressing a brother officer. "Have you any parents, either of you two?"

"No, Sir," rejoicingly from Lew and Jakin. "We're both orphans, Sir. There's no one to be considered of on our account, Sir."

"You poor little sprats, and you want to go up to the Front with the Regiment, do you? Why?"

"I've wore the Queen's Uniform for two years," said Jakin. "It's very 'ard, Sir, that a man don't get no recompense for doin' of 'is dooty, Sir."

"An'—an' if I don't go, Sir," interrupted Lew, "the Bandmaster 'e says 'e'll catch an' make a bloo—a blessed musician o' me, Sir. Before I've seen any service, Sir."

The Colonel made no answer for a long time. Then he said quietly: "If you're passed by the Doctor I dare say you can go. I shouldn't smoke if I were you."

The boys saluted and disappeared. The Colonel walked home and told the story to his wife, who nearly cried over it. The Colonel was well pleased. If that was the temper of the children, what would not the men do?

Jakin and Lew entered the boys' barrack-room with great stateliness, and refused to hold any conversation with their comrades for at least ten minutes. Then, bursting with pride, Jakin drawled: "I've bin intervooin' the Colonel. Good old beggar is the Colonel. Says I to 'im, 'Colonel,' says I, 'let me go to the Front, along o' the Reg'ment.—'To the Front you shall go,' says 'e, 'an' I only wish there was more like you among the dirty little devils that bang the bloomin' drums.' Kidd, if you throw your 'courtements at me for tellin' you the truth to your own advantage, your legs'll swell."

None the less there was a Battle-Royal in the barrack-room, for the boys were consumed with envy and hate, and neither Jakin nor Lew behaved in conciliatory wise.

"I'm goin' out to say adoo to my girl," said Lew, to cap the climax. "Don't none o' you touch my kit because it's wanted for active service; me bein' specially invited to go by the Colonel."

He strolled forth and whistled in the clump of trees at the back of the Married Quarters till Cris came to him, and, the preliminary kisses being given and taken, Lew began to explain the situation.

"I'm goin' to the Front with the Reg'ment," he said valiantly.

"Piggy, you're a little liar," said Cris, but her heart misgave her, for Lew was not in the habit of lying.

"Liar yourself, Cris," said Lew, slipping an arm round her. "I'm goin'. When the Reg'ment marches out you'll see me with 'em, all galliant and gay. Give us another kiss, Cris, on the strength of it."

"If you'd on'y a-stayed at the Depôt—where you ought to ha' bin—you could get as many of 'em as—as you dam please," whimpered Cris, putting up her mouth.

"It's 'ard, Cris. I grant you it's 'ard, But what's a man to do? If I'd a-stayed at the Depôt, you wouldn't think anything of me."

"Like as not, but I'd 'ave you with me, Piggy. An' all the thinkin' in the world isn't like kissin'.'"

"An' all the kissin' in the world isn't like 'avin' a medal to wear on the front o' your coat."

"You won't get no medal."

"Oh, yus, I shall though. Me an' Jakin are the only acting-drummers that'll be took along. All the rest is full men, an' we'll get our medals with them."

"They might ha' taken anybody but you, Piggy. You'll get killed—you're so venturesome. Stay with me, Piggy darlin', down at the Depôt, an' I'll love you true, for ever."

"Ain't you goin' to do that now, Cris? You said you was."

"O' course I am, but th' other's more comfortable. Wait till you've growed a bit, Piggy. You aren't no taller than me now."

"I've bin in the Army for two years, an' I'm not goin' to get out of a chanst o' seein' service, an' don't you try to make me do so. I'll come back, Cris, an' when I take on as a man I'll marry you—marry you when I'm a Lance."

"Promise, Piggy."

Lew reflected on the future as arranged by Jakin a short time previously, but Cris's mouth was very near to his own.

"I promise, s'elp me Gawd!" said he.

Cris slid an arm round his neck.

"I won't 'old you back no more, Piggy. Go away an' get your medal, an' I'll make you a new button-bag as nice as I know how," she whispered.

"Put some o' your 'air into it, Cris, an' I'll keep it in my pocket so long's I'm alive."

Then Cris wept anew, and the interview ended. Public feeling among the drummer-boys rose to fever pitch, and the lives of Jakin and Lew became unenviable. Not only had they been permitted to enlist two years before the regulation boy's age—fourteen—but, by virtue, it seemed, of their extreme youth, they were allowed to go to the Front—which thing had not happened to acting-drummers within the knowledge of boy. The Band which was to accompany the Regiment had been cut down to the regulation twenty men, the surplus returning to the ranks. Jakin and Lew were attached to the Band as supernumeraries, though they would much have preferred being company buglers.

"Don't matter much," said Jakin after the medical inspection. "Be thankful that we're 'lowed to go at all. The Doctor 'e said that if we could stand what we took from the Bazar-Sergeant's son we'd stand pretty nigh anything."

"Which we will," said Lew, looking tenderly at the ragged and ill- made housewife that Cris had given him, with a lock of her hair worked into a sprawling "L" upon the cover.

"It was the best I could," she sobbed. "I wouldn't let mother nor the Sergeant's tailor 'elp me. Keep it always, Piggy, an' remember I love you true."

They marched to the railway station, nine hundred and sixty strong, and every soul in cantonments turned out to see them go. The drummers gnashed their teeth at Jakin and Lew marching with the Band, the married women wept upon the platform, and the Regiment cheered its noble self black in the face.

"A nice level lot," said the Colonel to the Second-in-Command as they watched the first four companies entraining.

"Fit to do anything," said the Second-in-Command enthusiastically. "But it seems to me they're a thought too young and tender for the work in hand. It's bitter cold up at the Front now."

"They're sound enough," said the Colonel. "We must take our chance of sick casualties."

So they went northward, ever northward, past droves and droves of camels, armies of camp-followers, and legions of laden mules, the throng thickening day by day, till with a shriek the train pulled up at a hopelessly congested junction where six lines of temporary track accommodated six forty-waggon trains; where whistles blew, Babus sweated, and Commissariat officers swore from dawn till far into the night, amid the wind-driven chaff of the fodder-bales and the lowing of a thousand steers.

"Hurry up—you're badly wanted at the Front," was the message that greeted the Fore and Aft, and the occupants of the Red Cross carriages told the same tale.

"'Tisn't so much the bloomin' fightin'," gasped a head-bound trooper of Hussars to a knot of admiring Fore and Afts. "'Tisn't so much the bloomin' fightin', though there's enough o' that. It's the bloomin' food an' the bloomin' climate. Frost all night 'cept when it hails, and b'iling sun all day, and the water stinks fit to knock you down. I got my 'ead chipped like a egg; I've got pneumonia too, an' my guts is all out o' order. 'Tain't no bloomin' picnic in those parts, I can tell you."

"Wot are the niggers like?" demanded a private.

"There's some prisoners in that train yonder. Go an' look at 'em. They're the aristocracy o' the country. The common folk are a dashed sight uglier. If you want to know what they fight with, reach under my seat an' pull out the long knife that's there."

They dragged out and beheld for the first time the grim, bone- handled, triangular Afghan knife. It was almost as long as Lew.

"That's the thing to jint ye," said the trooper feebly. "It can take off a man's arm at the shoulder as easy as slicing butter. I halved the beggar that used that un, but there's more of his likes up above. They don't understand thrustin', but they're devils to slice."

The men strolled across the tracks to inspect the Afghan prisoners. They were unlike any "niggers" that the Fore and Aft had ever met—these huge, black-haired, scowling sons of the Beni-Israel. As the men stared the Afghans spat freely and muttered one to another with lowered eyes.

"My eyes! Wot awful swine!" said Jakin, who was in the rear of the procession. "Say, ole man, how you got puckrowed, eh? Kiswasti you wasn't hanged for your ugly face, hey?"

The tallest of the company turned, his leg-irons clanking at the movement, and stared at the boy. "See!" he cried to his fellows in Pushto. "They send children against us. What a people, and what fools!"

"Hya." said Jakin, nodding his head cheerily. "You go down-country. Khana get, peenikapanee get—live like a bloomin' Raja ke marfik. That's a better bandobust than baynit get it in your innards. Good-bye, ole man. Take care o' your beautiful figure- 'ead, an' try to look kushy."

The men laughed and fell in for their first march, when they began to realise that a soldier's life is not all beer and skittles. They were much impressed with the size and bestial ferocity of the niggers whom they had now learned to call "Paythans," and more with the exceeding discomfort of their own surroundings. Twenty old soldiers in the corps would have taught them how to make themselves moderately snug at night, but they had no old soldiers, and, as the troops on the line of march said, "they lived like pigs." They learned the heart-breaking cussedness of camp-kitchens and camels and the depravity of an E.P. tent and a wither-wrung mule. They studied animalculae in water, and developed a few cases of dysentery in their study.

At the end of their third march they were disagreeably surprised by the arrival in their camp of a hammered iron slug which, fired from a steady rest at seven hundred yards, flicked out the brains of a private seated by the fire. This robbed them of their peace for a night, and was the beginning of a long-range fire carefully calculated to that end. In the daytime they saw nothing except an unpleasant puff of smoke from a crag above the line of march. At night there were distant spurts of flame and occasional casualties, which set the whole camp blazing into the gloom and, occasionally, into opposite tents. Then they swore vehemently and vowed that this was magnificent but not war.

Indeed it was not. The Regiment could not halt for reprisals against the sharpshooters of the country-side. Its duty was to go forward and make connectioon with the Scotch and Gurkha troops with which it was brigaded. The Afghans knew this, and knew too, after their first tentative shots, that they were dealing with a raw regiment Thereafter they devoted themselves to the task of keeping the Fore and Aft on the strain. Not for anything would they have taken equal liberties with a seasoned corps—with the wicked little Gurkhas, whose delight it was to lie out in the open on a dark night and stalk their stalkers—with the terrible big men dressed in women's clothes, who could be heard praying to their God in the night-watches, and whose peace of mind no amount of "sniping" could shake—or with those vile Sikhs, who marched so ostentatiously unprepared and who dealt out such grim reward to those who tried to profit by that unpreparedness. This white regiment was different—quite different. It slept like a hog, and, like a hog, charged in every direction when it was roused. Its sentries walked with a footfall that could be heard for a quarter of a mile; would fire at anything that moved—even a driven donkey— and when they had once fired, could be scientifically "rushed " and laid out a horror and an offence against the morning sun. Then there were camp-followers who straggled and could be cut up without fear. Their shrieks would disturb the white boys, and the loss of their services would inconvenience them sorely.

Thus, at every march, the hidden enemy became bolder and the Regiment writhed and twisted under attacks it could not avenge. The crowning triumph was a sudden night-rush ending in the cutting of many tent-ropes, the collapse of the sodden canvas, and a glorious knifing of the men who struggled and kicked below. It was a great deed, neatly carried out, and it shook the already shaken nerves of the Fore and Aft. All the courage that they had been required to exercise up to this point was the "two o'clock in the morning courage"; and, so far, they had only succeeded in shooting their comrades and losing their sleep.

Sullen, discontented, cold, savage, sick, with their uniforms dulled and unclean, the Fore and Aft joined their Brigade.

"I hear you had a tough time of it coming up," said the Brigadier. But when he saw the hospital-sheets his face fell.

"This is bad," said he to himself. "They're as rotten as sheep." And aloud to the Colonel—"I'm afraid we can't spare you just yet. We want all we have, else I should have given you ten days to recover in."

The Colonel winced. "On my honour, Sir," he returned, "there is not the least necessity to think of sparing us. My men have been rather mauled and upset without a fair return. They only want to go in somewhere where they can see what's before them."

"Can't say I think much of the Fore and Fit," said the Brigadier in confidence to his Brigade-Major. "They've lost all their soldiering, and, by the trim of them, might have marched through the country from the other side. A more fagged-out set of men I never put eyes on."

"Oh, they'll improve as the work goes on. The parade gloss has been rubbed off a little, but they'll put on field polish before long," said the Brigade-Major. "They've been mauled, and they don't quite understand it."

They did not. All the hitting was on one side, and it was cruelly hard hitting with accessories that made them sick. There was also the real sickness that laid hold of a strong man and dragged him howling to the grave. Worst of all, their officers knew just as little of the country as the men themselves, and looked as if they did. The Fore and Aft were in a thoroughly unsatisfactory condition, but they believed that all would be well if they could once get a fair go-in at the enemy. Pot-shots up and down the valleys were unsatisfactory, and the bayonet never seemed to get a chance. Perhaps it was as well, for a long-limbed Afghan with a knife had a reach of eight feet, and could carry away lead that would disable three Englishmen.

The Fore and Aft would like some rifle-practice at the enemy—all seven hundred rifles blazing together. That wish showed the mood of the men.

The Gurkhas walked into their camp, and in broken, barrack-room English strove to fraternise with them: offered them pipes of tobacco and stood them treat at the canteen. But the Fore and Aft, not knowing much of the nature of the Gurkhas, treated them as they would treat any other "niggers," and the little men in green trotted back to their firm friends the Highlanders, and with many grins confided to them: "That dam white regiment no dam use. Sulky—ugh! Dirty—ugh! Hya, any tot for Johnny?" Whereat the Highlanders smote the Gurkhas as to the head, and told them not to vilify a British Regiment, and the Gurkhas grinned cavernously, for the Highlanders were their elder brothers and entitled to the privileges of kinship. The common soldier who touches a Gurkha is more than likely to have his head sliced open.

Three days later the Brigadier arranged a battle according to the rules of war and the peculiarity of the Afghan temperament. The enemy were massing in inconvenient strength among the hills, and the moving of many green standards warned him that the tribes were "up" in aid of the Afghan regular troops. A squadron and a half of Bengal Lancers represented the available Cavalry, and two screw-guns, borrowed from a column thirty miles away, the Artillery at the General's disposal.

"If they stand, as I've a very strong notion that they will, I fancy we shall see an infantry fight that will be worth watching," said the Brigadier. "We'll do it in style. Each regiment shall be played into action by its Band, and we'll hold the Cavalry in reserve."

"For all the reserve?" somebody asked.

"For all the reserve; because we're going to crumple them up," said the Brigadier, who was an extraordinary Brigadier, and did not believe in the value of a reserve when dealing with Asiatics. Indeed, when you come to think of it, had the British Army consistently waited for reserves in all its little affairs, the boundaries of Our Empire would have stopped at Brighton beach.

The battle was to be a glorious battle.

The three regiments debouching from three separate gorges, after duly crowning the heights above, were to converge from the centre, left, and right upon what we will call the Afghan army, then stationed towards the lower extremity of a flat-bottomed valley. Thus it will be seen that three sides of the valley practically belonged to the English, while the fourth was strictly Afghan property. In the event of defeat the Afghans had the rocky hills to fly to, where the fire from the guerrilla tribes in aid would cover their retreat. In the event of victory these same tribes would rush down and lend their weight to the rout of the British.

The screw-guns were to shell the head of each Afghan rush that was made in close formation, and the Cavalry, held in reserve in the right valley, were to gently stimulate the break-up which would follow on the combined attack. The Brigadier, sitting upon a rock overlooking the valley, would watch the battle unrolled at his feet. The Fore and Aft would debouch from the central gorge, the Gurkhas from the left, and the Highlanders from the right, for the reason that the left flank of the enemy seemed as though it required the most hammering. It was not every day that an Afghan force would take ground in the open, and the Brigadier was resolved to make the most of it.

"If we only had a few more men," he said plaintively, "we could surround the creatures and crumple 'em up thoroughly. As it is, I'm afraid we can only cut them up as they run. It's a great pity."

The Fore and Aft had enjoyed unbroken peace for five days, and were beginning, in spite of dysentery, to recover their nerve. But they were not happy, for they did not know the work in hand, and had they known, would not have known how to do it. Throughout those five days in which old soldiers might have taught them the craft of the game, they discussed together their misadventures in the past—how such an one was alive at dawn and dead ere the dusk, and with what shrieks and struggles such another had given up his soul under the Afghan knife. Death was a new and horrible thing to the sons of mechanics who were used to die decently of zymotic disease; and their careful conservation in barracks had done nothing to make them look upon it with less dread.

Very early in the dawn the bugles began to blow, and the Fore and Aft, filled with a misguided enthusiasm, turned out without waiting for a cup of coffee and a biscuit; and were rewarded by being kept under arms in the cold while the other regiments leisurely prepared for the fray. All the world knows that it is ill taking the breeks off a Highlander. It is much iller to try to make him stir unless he is convinced of the necessity for haste.

The Fore and Aft waited, leaning upon their rifles and listening to the protests of their empty stomachs. The Colonel did his best to remedy the default of lining as soon as it was borne in upon him that the affair would not begin at once, and so well did he succeed that the coffee was just ready when—the men moved off, their Band leading. Even then there had been a mistake in time, and the Fore and Aft came out into the valley ten minutes before the proper hour. Their Band wheeled to the right after reaching the open, and retired behind a little rocky knoll still playing while the Regiment went past.

It was not a pleasant sight that opened on the uninstructed view, for the lower end of the valley appeared to be filled by an army in position—real and actual regiments attired in red coats, and—of this there was no doubt—firing Martini-Henry bullets which cut up the ground a hundred yards in front of the leading company. Over that pock-marked ground the Regiment had to pass, and it opened the ball with a general and profound courtesy to the piping pickets; ducking in perfect time, as though it had been brazed on a rod. Being half capable of thinking for itself, it fired a volley by the simple process of pitching its rifle into its shoulder and pulling the trigger. The bullets may have accounted for some of the watchers on the hill side, but they certainly did not affect the mass of enemy in front, while the noise of the rifles drowned any orders that might have been given.

"Good God!" said the Brigadier, sitting on the rock high above all. "That Regiment has spoilt the whole show. Hurry up the others, and let the screw-guns get off."

But the screw-guns, in working round the heights, had stumbled upon a wasp's nest of a small mud fort which they incontinently shelled at eight hundred yards, to the huge discomfort of the occupants, who were unaccustomed to weapons of such devilish precision.

The Fore and Aft continued to go forward, but with shortened stride. Where were the other regiments, and why did these niggers use Martinis? They took open order instinctively, lying down and firing at random, rushing a few paces forward and lying down again, according to the regulations. Once in this formation, each man felt himself desperately alone, and edged in towards his fellow for comfort's sake.

Then the crack of his neighbor's rifle at his ear led him to fire as rapidly as he could—again for the sake of the comfort of the noise. The reward was not long delayed. Five volleys plunged the files in banked smoke impenetrable to the eye, and the bullets began to take ground twenty or thirty yards in front of the firers, as the weight of the bayonet dragged down and to the right arms wearied with holding the kick of the leaping Martini. The Company Commanders peered helplessly through the smoke, the more nervous mechanically trying to fan it away with their helmets.

"High and to the left!" bawled a Captain till he was hoarse. "No good! Cease firing, and let it drift away a bit."

Three and four times the bugles shrieked the order, and when it was obeyed the Fore and Aft looked that their foe should be lying before them in mown swaths of men. A light wind drove the smoke to leeward, and showed the enemy still in position and apparently unaffected. A quarter of a ton of lead had been buried a furlong in front of them, as the ragged earth attested.

That was not demoralizing to the Afghans, who have not European nerves. They were waiting for the mad riot to die down, and were firing quietly into the heart of the smoke. A private of the Fore and Aft spun up his company shrieking with agony, another was kicking the earth and gasping, and a third, ripped through the lower intestines by a jagged bullet, was calling aloud on his comrades to put him out of his pain. These were the casualties, and they were not soothing to hear or see. The smoke cleared to a dull haze.

Then the foe began to shout with a great shouting, and a mass—a black mass—detached itself from the main body, and rolled over the ground at horrid speed. It was composed of, perhaps, three hundred men, who would shout and fire and slash if the rush of their fifty comrades who were determined to die carried home. The fifty were Ghazis, half maddened with drugs and wholly mad with religious fanaticism. When they rushed the British fire ceased, and in the lull the order was given to close ranks and meet them with the bayonet.

Any one who knew the business could have told the Fore and Aft that the only way of dealing with a Ghazi rush is by volleys at long ranges; because a man who means to die, who desires to die, who will gain heaven by dying, must, in nine cases out of ten, kill a man who has a lingering prejudice in favour of life. Where they should have closed and gone forward, the Fore and Aft opened out and skirmished, and where they should have opened out and fired, they closed and waited.

A man dragged from his blankets half awake and unfed is never in a pleasant frame of mind. Nor does his happiness increase when he watches the whites of the eyes of three hundred six-foot fiends upon whose beards the foam is lying, upon whose tongues is a roar of wrath, and in whose hands are yard-long knives.

The Fore and Aft heard the Gurkha bugles bringing that regiment forward at the double, while the neighing of the Highland pipes came from the left. They strove to stay where they were, though the bayonets wavered down the line like the oars of a ragged boat. Then they felt body to body the amazing physical strength of their foes; a shriek of pain ended the rush, and the knives fell amid scenes not to be told. The men clubbed together and smote blindly—as often as not at their own fellows. Their front crumpled like paper, and the fifty Ghazis passed on; their backers, now drunk with success, fighting as madly as they.

Then the rear ranks were bidden to close up, and the subalterns dashed into the stew—alone. For the rear-ranks had heard the clamour in front, the yells and the howls of pain, and had seen the dark stale blood that makes afraid. They were not going to stay. It was the rushing of the camps over again. Let their officers go to Hell, if they chose; they would get away from the knives.

"Come on!" shrieked the subalterns, and their men, cursing them, drew back, each closing in to his neighbour and wheeling round.

Charteris and Devlin, subalterns of the last company, faced their death alone in the belief that their men would follow.

"You've killed me, you cowards," sobbed Devlin and dropped, cut from the shoulder-strap to the centre of the chest; and a fresh detachment of his men retreating, always retreating, trampled him under foot as they made for the pass whence they had emerged.

I kissed her in the kitchen and I kissed her in the hall
      Child'un, child'un, follow me!
'Oh Golly,' said the cook, 'is he gwine to kiss us all?'
      Halla—Halla—Halla—Hallelujah!

The Gurkhas were pouring through the left gorge and over the heights at the double to the invitation of their Regimental Quick-step. The black rocks were crowned with dark green spiders as the bugles gave tongue jubilantly:—

In the morning! In the morning by the bright light!
When Gabriel blows his trumpet in the morning!

The Gurkha rear companies tripped and blundered over loose stones. The front files halted for a moment to take stock of the valley and to settle stray boot-laces. Then a happy little sigh of contentment soughed down the ranks, and it was as though the land smiled, for behold there below was the enemy, and it was to meet them that the Gurkhas had doubled so hastily. There was much enemy. There would be amusement. The little men hitched their kukris well to hand, and gaped expectantly at their officers as terriers grin ere the stone is cast for them to fetch. The Gurkhas' ground sloped downward to the valley, and they enjoyed a fair view of the proceedings. They sat upon the boulders to watch, for their officers were not going to waste their wind in assisting to repulse a Ghazi rush more than half a mile away. Let the white men look to their own front.

"Hi! yi!" said the Subadar-Major, who was sweating profusely. "Dam fools yonder, stand close order! This is no time for close order, it is the time for volleys. Ugh!"

Horrified, amused, and indignant, the Gurkhas beheld the retirement of the Fore and Aft with a running chorus of oaths and commentaries.

"They run! The white men run! Colonel Sahib, may we also do a little running?" murmured Runbir Thappa, the Senior Jemadar.

But the Colonel would have none of it. "Let the beggars be cut up a little," said he wrathfully. "Serves 'em right. They'll be prodded into facing round in a minute." He looked through his field-glasses, and caught the glint of an officer's sword.

"Beating 'em with the flat—damned conscripts! How the Ghazis are walking into them!" said he.

The Fore and Aft, heading back, bore with them their officers. The narrowness of the pass forced the mob into solid formation, and the rear ranks delivered some sort of a wavering volley. The Ghazis drew off, for they did not know what reserve the gorge might hide. Moreover, it was never wise to chase white men too far. They returned as wolves return to cover, satisfied with the slaughter that they had done, and only stopping to slash at the wounded on the ground. A quarter of a mile had the Fore and Aft retreated, and now, jammed in the pass, was quivering with pain, shaken and demoralised with fear, while the officers, maddened beyond control, smote the men with the hilts and the flats of their swords.

"Get back! Get back, you cowards—you women! Right about face—column of companies, form—you hounds!" shouted the Colonel, and the subalterns swore aloud. But the Regiment wanted to go—to go anywhere out of the range of those merciless knives. It swayed to and fro irresolutely with shouts and outcries, while from the right the Gurkhas dropped volley after volley of cripple-stopper Snider bullets at long range into the mob of the Ghazis returning to their own troops.

The Fore and Aft Band, though protected from direct fire by the rocky knoll under which it had sat down, fled at the first rush. Jakin and Lew would have fled also, but their short legs left them fifty yards in the rear, and by the time the Band had mixed with the Regiment, they were painfully aware that they would have to close in alone and unsupported.

"Get back to that rock," gasped Jakin. "They won't see us there."

And they returned to the scattered instruments of the Band, their hearts nearly bursting their ribs.

"Here's a nice show for us," said Jakin, throwing himself full length on the ground. "A bloomin' fine show for British Infantry! Oh, the devils! They've gone and left us alone here! Wot'll we do?"

Lew took possession of a cast-off water-bottle, which naturally was full of canteen rum, and drank till he coughed again.

"Drink," said he shortly. "They'll come back in a minute or two—you see."

Jakin drank, but there was no sign of the Regiment's return. They could hear a dull clamour from the head of the valley of retreat, and saw the Ghazis slink back, quickening their pace as the Gurkhas fired at them.

"We're all that's left of the Band, an' we'll be cut up as sure as death," said Jakin.

"I'll die game, then," said Lew thickly, fumbling with his tiny drummer's sword. The drink was working on his brain as it was on Jakin's.

"'Old on! I know something better than fightin'," said Jakin, stung by the splendour of a sudden thought due chiefly to rum. "Tip our bloomin' cowards yonder the word to come back. The Paythan beggars are well away. Come on, Lew! We won't get hurt. Take the fife an' give me the drum. The Old Step for all your bloomin' guts are worth! There's a few of our men coming back now. Stand up, ye drunken little defaulter. By your right—quick march!"

He slipped the drum-sling over his shoulder, thrust the fife into Lew's hand, and the two boys marched out of the cover of the rock into the open, making a hideous hash of the first bars of the "British Grenadiers."

As Lew had said, a few of the Fore and Aft were coming back sullenly and shamefacedly under the stimulus of blows and abuse; their red coats shone at the head of the valley, and behind them were wavering bayonets. But between this shattered line and the enemy, who with Afghan suspicion feared that the hasty retreat meant an ambush, and had not moved therefore, lay half a mile of level ground dotted only by the wounded.

The tune settled into full swing and the boys kept shoulder to shoulder, Jakin banging the drum as one possessed. The one fife made a thin and pitiful squeaking, but the tune carried far, even to the Gurkhas.

"Come on, you dorgs!" muttered Jakin to himself. "Are we to play for hever?" Lew was staring straight in front of him and marching more stiffly than ever he had done on parade.

And in bitter mockery of the distant mob, the old tune of the Old Line shrilled and rattled:—

Some talk of Alexander,
    And some of Hercules;
Of Hector and Lysander,
And such great names as these!

There was a far-off clapping of hands from the Gurkhas, and a roar from the Highlanders in the distance, but never a shot was fired by British or Afghan. The two little red dots moved forward in the open parallel to the enemy's front.

But of all the world's great heroes
    There's none that can compare,
With a tow-row-row-row-row-row,
    To the British Grenadier!

The men of the Fore and Aft were gathering thick at the entrance into the plain. The Brigadier on the heights far above was speechless with rage. Still no movement from the enemy. The day stayed to watch the children.

Jakin halted and beat the long roll of the Assembly, while the fife squealed despairingly.

"Right about face! Hold up, Lew, you're drunk," said Jakin. They wheeled and marched back:—

Those heroes of antiquity
    Ne'er saw a cannon-ball,
Nor knew the force o' powder,

"Here they come!" said Jakin. "Go on, Lew":—

To scare their foes withal!

The Fore and Aft were pouring out of the valley. What officers had said to men in that time of shame and humiliation will never be known; for neither officers nor men speak of it now.

"They are coming anew!" shouted a priest among the Afghans. "Do not kill the boys! Take them alive, and they shall be of our faith."

But the first volley had been fired, and Lew dropped on his face. Jakin stood for a minute, spun round and collapsed, as the Fore and Aft came forward, the curses of their officers in their ears, and in their hearts the shame of open shame.

Half the men had seen the drummers die, and they made no sign. They did not even shout. They doubled out straight across the plain in open order, and they did not fire.

"This," said the Colonel of Gurkhas, softly, "is the real attack, as it should have been delivered. Come on, my children."

"Ulu-lu-lu-lu!" squealed the Gurkhas, and came down with a joyful clicking of kukris—those vicious Gurkha knives.

On the right there was no rush. The Highlanders, cannily commending their souls to God (for it matters as much to a dead man whether he has been shot in a Border scuffle or at Waterloo), opened out and fired according to their custom, that is to say without heat and without intervals, while the screw-guns, having disposed of the impertinent mud fort aforementioned, dropped shell after shell into the clusters round the flickering green standards on the heights.

"Charrging is an unfortunate necessity," murmured the Colour- Sergeant of the right company of the Highlanders. "It makes the men sweer so—but I am thinkin' that it will come to a charrge if these black devils stand much longer. Stewarrt, man, you're firing into the eye of the sun, and he'll not take any harm for Government ammuneetion. A foot lower and a great deal slower! What are the English doing? They're very quiet, there in the center. Running again?"

The English were not running. They were hacking and hewing and stabbing, for though one white man is seldom physically a match for an Afghan in a sheepskin or wadded coat, yet, through the pressure of many white men behind, and a certain thirst for revenge in his heart, he becomes capable of doing much with both ends of his rifle. The Fore and Aft held their fire till one bullet could drive through five or six men, and the front of the Afghan force gave on the volley. They then selected their men, and slew them with deep gasps and short hacking coughs, and groanings of leather belts against strained bodies, and realised for the first time that an Afghan attacked is far less formidable than an Afghan attacking; which fact old soldiers might have told them.

But they had no old soldiers in their ranks.

The Gurkhas' stall at the bazar was the noisiest, for the men were engaged—to a nasty noise as of beef being cut on the block—with the kukri, which they preferred to the bayonet; well knowing how the Afghan hates the half-moon blade.

As the Afghans wavered, the green standards on the mountain moved down to assist them in a last rally. This was unwise. The Lancers, chafing in the right gorge, had thrice despatched their only subaltern as galloper to report on the progress of affairs. On the third occasion he returned, with a bullet-graze on his knee, swearing strange oaths in Hindustani, and saying that all things were ready. So that squadron swung round the right of the Highlanders with a wicked whistling of wind in the pennons of its lances, and fell upon the remnant just when, according to all the rules of war, it should have waited for the foe to show more signs of wavering.

But it was a dainty charge, deftly delivered, and it ended by the Cavalry finding itself at the head of the pass by which the Afghans intended to retreat; and down the track that the lances had made streamed two companies of the Highlanders, which was never intended by the Brigadier. The new development was successful. It detached the enemy from his base as a sponge is torn from a rock, and left him ringed about with fire in that pitiless plain. And as a sponge is chased round the bath-tub by the hand of the bather, so were the Afghans chased till they broke into little detachments much more difficult to dispose of than large masses.

"See!" quoth the Brigadier. "Everything has come as I arranged. We've cut their base, and now we'll bucket 'em to pieces."

A direct hammering was all that the Brigadier had dared to hope for, considering the size of the force at his disposal; but men who stand or fall by the errors of their opponents may be forgiven for turning Chance into Design. The bucketing went forward merrily. The Afghan forces were upon the run—the run of wearied wolves who snarl and bite over their shoulders. The red lances dipped by twos and threes, and, with a shriek, uprose the lance-butt, like a spar on a stormy sea, as the trooper cantering forward cleared his point. The Lancers kept between their prey and the steep hills, for all who could were trying to escape from the valley of death. The Highlanders gave the fugitives two hundred yards' law, and then brought them down, gasping and choking ere they could reach the protection of the boulders above. The Gurkhas followed suit; but the Fore and Aft were killing on their own account, for they had penned a mass of men between their bayonets and a wall of rock, and the flash of the rifles was lighting the wadded coats.

"We cannot hold them, Captain Sahib!" panted a Ressaidar of Lancers. "Let us try the carbine. The lance is good, but it wastes time."

They tried the carbine, and still the enemy melted away—fled up the hills by hundreds when there were only twenty bullets to stop them. On the heights the screw-guns ceased firing—they had run out of ammunition—and the Brigadier groaned, for the musketry fire could not sufficiently smash the retreat. Long before the last volleys were fired, the doolies were out in force looking for the wounded. The battle was over, and, but for want of fresh troops, the Afghans would have been wiped off the earth. As it was, they counted their dead by hundreds, and nowhere were the dead thicker than in the track of the Fore and Aft.

But the Regiment did not cheer with the Highlanders, nor did they dance uncouth dances with the Gurkhas among the dead. They looked under their brows at the Colonel as they leaned upon their rifles and panted.

"Get back to camp, you. Haven't you disgraced yourself enough for one day! Go and look to the wounded. It's all you're fit for," said the Colonel. Yet for the past hour the Fore and Aft had been doing all that mortal commander could expect. They had lost heavily because they did not know how to set about their business with proper skill, but they had borne themselves gallantly, and this was their reward.

A young and sprightly Colour-Sergeant, who had begun to imagine himself a hero, offered his water-bottle to a Highlander whose tongue was black with thirst. "I drink with no cowards," answered the youngster huskily, and, turning to a Gurkha, said, "Hya, Johnny! Drink water got it?" The Gurkha grinned and passed his bottle. The Fore and Aft said no word.

They went back to camp when the field of strife had been a little mopped up and made presentable, and the Brigadier, who saw himself a Knight in three months, was the only soul who was complimentary to them. The Colonel was heartbroken, and the officers were savage and sullen.

"Well," said the Brigadier, "they are young troops, of course, and it was not unnatural that they should retire in disorder for a bit."

"Oh, my only Aunt Maria! " murmured a junior Staff Officer. "Retire in disorder! It was a bally run!"

"But they came again, as we all know," cooed the Brigadier, the Colonel's ashy-white face before him, "and they behaved as well as could possibly be expected. Behaved beautifully, indeed. I was watching them. It's not a matter to take to heart, Colonel. As some German General said of his men, they wanted to be shooted over a little, that was all." To himself he said—"Now they're blooded I can give 'em responsible work. It's as well that they got what they did. Teach 'em more than half a dozen rifle flirtations, that will—later—run alone and bite. Poor old Colonel, though."

All that afternoon the heliograph winked and flickered on the hills, striving to tell the good news to a mountain forty miles away And in the evening there arrived, dusty, sweating, and sore, a misguided Correspondent who had gone out to assist at a trumpery village-burning, and who had read off the message from afar, cursing his luck the while.

"Let's have the details somehow—as full as ever you can, please. It's the first time I've ever been left this campaign," said the Correspondent to the Brigadier; and the Brigadier, nothing loth, told him how an Army of Communication had been crumpled up, destroyed, and all but annihilated by the craft, strategy, wisdom, and foresight of the Brigadier.

But some say, and among these be the Gurkhas who watched on the hillside, that that battle was won by Jakin and Lew, whose little bodies were borne up just in time to fit two gaps at the head of the big ditch-grave for the dead under the heights of Jagai.

Rudyard Kipling – A Short Biography

Born in Bombay on 30th December 1865, Joseph Rudyard Kipling wrote short stories, poems and novels, a body of work whose reputation is in constant flux as his presentations and interpretations of empire are viewed within the changing context of empirical absolution in the twentieth century. Having spent the first five years of his life in India he felt a natural affinity for the country, though his upbringing had a distinctly colonial taste flavour. He was born in the Bombay Presidency of British India to Lockwood Kipling, an English art teacher and illustrator who took a position as professor of architectural sculpture in the Jeejeebhoy School of Art and Alice MacDonald, spoken of by the a Viceroy of India that "dullness and Mrs Kipling cannot exist in the same room". Though their presence in India was principally artistic and educational, rather than political, the company they kept and the establishments in which they kept it indicate an existence very much benefitting from the British Empire. Lockwood would later go on to assume a position as curator of the Lahore Museum, while working on various illustrations for Rudyard's writing, and various decorations for the Victoria and Albert museum in London. Much of his work, then, was coloured by the empire, whether in service to or benefitting from, and it was into this distinctly British experience of India that Rudyard was born.

Lockwood and Alice had met and fallen in love at Rudyard Lake in Rudyard, Staffordshire, and their affections for the area were so great they chose to refer to the lake in naming their first-born. Alice came from a family of four sisters, all of whose marriages were significant and well-arranged; moreover, Rudyard's most famous relative was Stanley Baldwin, Conservative Prime Minister on three occasions in the 1920s and 1930s. Kipling's sense of belonging in Bombay is found in 'To the City of Bombay' in the dedication to Seven Seas, a collection of poems published in 1900, which reads:—

> Mother of Cities to me,
> For I was born in her gate,
> Between the palms and the sea,
> Where the world-end steamers wait.

His parents considered themselves Anglo-Indians, and he would later assume this classification although he did not live there long. His first five years, which he describes as days of "strong light and darkness", ended when he and his three-year-old sister Alice were removed to Southsea, Plymouth, to board with Captain Pryse Agar Holloway and his wife Mrs Sarah Holloway, a couple who cared for the children of couples born in British India. They were there for six years and Kipling would later recall their time there with horror, describing incidents of cruelty and neglect and wondering whether it was these which speeded up his literary maturity, for "it made me give attention to the lies I soon found it necessary to tell: and this, I presume, is the foundation of literary effort".

Alice's time, by contrast, was relatively comfortable, Mrs Holloway hoping that she would marry her son, though this ambition would not come to fruition. They did have relatives in England, a maternal aunt Georgiana and her husband who lived in Fulham, London, in a house at which they spent a month each Christmas and which Kipling later described as "a paradise which I verily believe saved me". Their mother returned in 1877 and removed them from their custody with the Holloways. A year later he gained admission to the United Services College at Westward Ho! in Devon, a recently established school with the intention of readying boys for military service in the British Army. His time here was fraught physically, though emotionally it proved fruitful for he began several firm friendships with other boys at the school. Moreover, he found in it inspiration for the setting of his series of schoolboy stories, Stalky and Co, begun in 1899. Meanwhile, his sister Alice had returned to Southsea and was boarding with Florence Garrard, with whom he fell in love and on whom he modeled Maisie in his first novel, The Light That Failed, published in 1891. At sixteen he was found lacking in the academic perspicacity necessary to undertake a scholarship to Oxford University, his parents meanwhile lacking the wherewithal to finance him therein. As such his father sought a job for him in Lahore, Punjab, where he was now a museum curator. The position he found for his son was as assistant editor of the Civil and Military Gazette, a small local newspaper. Kipling left for India on 20th September 1882, arriving in Bombay on 18th October. "There were yet three or four days" rail to Lahore, where my people lived. After these, my English years fell away, nor ever, I think, came back in full strength".

The Gazette appeared six days of the week, year-round save for a short break at both Christmas and Easter. Its editor Stephen Wheeler was diligent but Kipling's writing was insatiable, and he came to consider the paper his "mistress and most true love". In the summer of 1883 Kipling visited Shimla, the colonial hill-station and summer capital of British India which was then called Simla. Chosen by the British owing to its resemblance of English climate and scenery (as far as was possible in India), it became the seat of the Viceroy of India for the six months on the plains which were too hot for the British temperament, and subsequently became a "centre of power as well as pleasure". Lockwood was asked to serve in the Church there, and his family became yearly visitors while Kipling himself would take his annual leave here from 1885-88. The value of this time is evident from the regularity with which Simla appears in his writing for the Gazette, which in his journals he describes the time as

> "….pure joy—every golden hour counted. It began in heat and discomfort, by rail and road. It ended in the cool evening, with a wood fire in one's bedroom, and next morn—thirty more of them ahead!—the early cup of tea, the Mother who brought it in, and the long talks of us all together again."

In 1886, his Departmental Ditties appeared, his first collection of verse, and brought with it a change of editor; Kay Robinson, Wheeler's replacement, was in favour of Kipling's creativity and granted him more freedom in that respect, even asking him to write short stories to appear in the newspaper. The vivacity of his writing was captured in a description of him by an ex-colleague at the Gazette, saying he "never knew such a fellow for ink—he simply revelled in it, filling up his pen viciously, and then throwing the contents all over the office, so that it was almost dangerous to approach him". While in Lahore, he had thirty-nine stories published in the Gazette between November 1886 and June 1887. Most of these are compiled in Plain Tales from the Hills, his first collection of prose, which was published in January 1888 in Calcutta, shortly after his 22nd birthday. In November 1887, he transferred from the Gazette to its much larger sister newspaper, The Pioneer, based in Allahabad. The pace of his writing remained, and in 1888 he published six collections of stories, Soldiers Three, The Story of the Gadsbys, In Black and White, Under the Deodars, The Phantom Rickshaw and Wee Willie Winkie, composed of some 41 stories. In addition, his position as The Pioneer's special correspondent in the Western region of Rajputna, he wrote many sketches which were later compiled in Letters of Marque and published in From Sea to Sea and Other Sketches, Letters of Travel.

A dispute in 1889 saw him discharged from The Pioneer, though by now he had been considering his future and sold the rights to his six volumes of stories for £200 and a small royalty, while the Plain Tales fetched £50, along with six months' salary from The Pioneer in lieu of notice. Using the money to undertake a pilgrimage to London, the literary centre of the British Empire, he left India on 9th March 1889, travelling via Rangoon, San Francisco, Hong Kong and Japan, then through the United States writing articles for The Pioneer which were also included in From Sea to Sea and Other Sketches, Letters of Travel. Arriving in England at Liverpool on October 1889, London and his literary début there beckoned.

His first task was to find a place to live, and he eventually settled on quarters in Villiers Street, Strand. The next two years saw several stories accepted by various magazine editors, the publication of the novel The Light That Failed, a nervous breakdown, the collaboration with Wolcott Balestier on the novel (uncharacteristically misspelt) The Naulhaka, and in 1891, following his doctors' advice, he embarked on a further sea voyage, travelling to South Africa, Australia, New Zealand and also returning to India. His plans to spend Christmas with his family were cut short on the news of Balestier's sudden death from typhoid fever, prompting an immediate return to London. Before he left, he had proposed to Balestier's sister Caroline Starr Balestier, with whom he had been having a hushed romance for just over a year. Back in London, Life's Handicap was published in 1891, a collection of short stories whose subject was the British in India, and British India. On 18th January 1892 aged 26 he married Caroline in the midst of an epidemic of influenza. Caroline was given away by Henry James, the famous and celebrated American author.

Honeymooning in Japan, they travelled via Vermont, America, to visit the Balestier estate, and upon arrival in Yokahama they found that their bank, The New Oriental Banking Corporation, had failed, though this loss did not deter them and they returned to Vermont, Caroline now pregnant with their first child. Renting a cottage on a farm for $10 per month, they lived a spartan existence and were "extraordinarily and self-centredly content". The named the residence Bliss Cottage, and it was here that the child was born, named Josephine, "in three foot of snow on the night of 29th December 1892. Her Mother's birthday being the 31st and mine the 30th we congratulated her on her sense of the fitness of things." While here, Kipling had his first ideas for the Jungle Books. Shortly after Josephine was born the couple moved in pursuit of more space and comfort, buying ten acres overlooking the Connecticut River from Caroline's brother. The house they built there was inspired by the Mughul architecture he encountered in Lahore, and was named Naulakha (this time correctly spelt) in honour of Wolcott. His literary output in four years here included the Jungle Books, a collection of short stories entitled The Day's Work, the novel Captain Courageous and a plethora of poetry, of which most notably the volume The Seven Seas and his Barrack-Room Ballads. Meanwhile, he enjoyed correspondence with the many children who wrote to him about the Jungle Books.

In between this writing, Kipling took regular visitors. Most notably Arthur Conan Doyle came, bringing golf clubs and staying for two days to give Kipling an extended golf lesson. Kipling enjoyed the game so much that he continued to play, even in winter with special red balls, though he found that the ice would lead to drives travelling two miles as they slid "down the long slope to the Connecticut River". Elsie, the couple's second daughter, was born in February 1896, and by this time it is thought that their marriage had lost its original spark of spontaneity and descended into routine, though they remained loyal to one another. By now, failed arbitration between the United States and England over a border dispute involving British Guiana incited Anglo-American tensions which, in May 1896, resulted in a confrontation between Kipling and Caroline's brother, resulting in his arrest and, in the hearing which followed, the destruction of Kipling's private life, leaving him exhausted and miserable and leading to their return to England.

They had settled Torquay, Devon, by September 1896, and he remained socially present and literarily productive. The success of his writing had brought him fame, and he had responded with a sense of duty to include in his writing elements of political persuasion, most notably in his two poems Recessional and The White Man's Burden, which caused controversy when they were published in 1897 and 1899 respectively. Many considered them anthemic to the empire, propaganda for the imperial mindset so prevalent in the Victoria era. Their first son, John, was born in August 1887. Another journey to South Africa began a tradition of wintering there, which continued until 1908. His reputation as Poet of the Empire saw him well-received by politicians in the Cape Colony, and he started the newspaper The Friend for Lord Roberts and the British troops in Bloemfontein. Back in England, they moved to Rottingdean, East Sussex, in 1897, and in 1902 he bought Bateman's, a house built in 1630, which was his home from until his death in 1936. Kim was published in 1902, after which he collected material for Just So Stories for Little Children, published a year later. Both he and Josephine developed pneumonia while visiting the United States, from which she later died.

This decade proved his most successful, being awarded the Nobel Prize for Literature in 1907, the prize citation reading "in consideration of the power of observation, originality of imagination, virility of ideas and remarkable talent for narration which characterise the creations of this world-famous author". He was the first English-language recipient. At the award ceremony in Switzerland, Carl David af Wirsén praised Kipling and the English literary tradition:

The Swedish Academy, in awarding the Nobel Prize in Literature this year to Rudyard Kipling, desires to pay a tribute to the literature of England, so rich in manifold glories, and to the greatest genius in the realm of narrative that that country has produced in our times.

Following this achievement, Kipling published Rewards and Fairies, which contained If, voted Britain's favourite poem in a BBC opinion poll in 1995. He turned down several recommendations for knighthood and was considered for Poet Laureate, though this position was never offered to him.

The sense of perseverance, honour and stoicism in If prevailed in many of his opinions, including that on the First World War. Writing in The New Army in Training in 1915, he scorned those who refused conscription, considering

> ....what will be the position in years to come of the young man who has deliberately elected to outcaste himself from this all-embracing brotherhood? What of his family, and, above all, what of his descendants, when the books have been closed and the last balance struck of sacrifice and sorrow in every hamlet, village, parish, suburb, city, shire, district, province, and Dominion throughout the Empire?

This attitude saw him encourage his son, John, to go to war, and he was promptly killed at the Battle of Loos in September 1915, aged 18. Last seen during the battle stumbling blindly through the mud, screaming in agony after an exploding shell had ripped his face apart, Kipling would write—

"If any question why we died
Tell them, because our fathers lied"

—perhaps betraying the guilt he felt at encouraging his son to go to war and finding him a position in the Irish Guards through his friendship with commander-in-chief Lord Roberts, for whom he had established The Friend in Bloemfontein. His death inspired much of Kipling's successive writing, notably My Boy Jack and a two-volume history of the Irish Guards, considered one of the finest examples of regimental history. Ironically, though his writing and his political position had arguably cost John his life, after the war he became friends with a French soldier whose copy of Kim, kept in his breast pocket, had stopped a bullet and saved his life. For a while the book and the soldier's Croix de Guerre were with Kipling, presented as tokens of gratitude, and they remained in contact, though when Kipling learned of the soldier's child he insisted on returning both book and medal.

He kept writing until 1930, though at a considerably slower pace, and to less success. His death, already once incorrectly announced early by a magazine in a premature obituary (and to which he responded "I've just read that I am dead. Don't forget to delete me from your list of subscribers") came on 18th January 1936, at the age of 70, from a perforated duodenal ulcer. His coffin was carried by, among others, his cousin the Prime Minister Stanley Baldwin, and his marble casket covered by a Union flag. He was cremated at Golders Green Crematorium in Northwest London and his ashes are buried at Poets' Corner in Westminster Abbey, alongside the graves of both Charles Dickens and Thomas Hardy.

In conjunction with various earthly memorials which commemorate him, alongside his extensive writing, he has a crater on Mercury named after him. The question of memorial and monument is much-addressed in English Literature and, as various great authors and poets have agreed before Kipling's time, his memory lives on more vivaciously set in his words, far longer and better represented than it could set in stone.

Rudyard Kipling - A Concise Bibliography

Books
The City of Dreadful Night (1885, short story)
Plain Tales from the Hills (1888)
Soldiers Three (1888)
The Story of the Gadsbys (1888)
In Black and White (1888)
Under the Deodars (1888)
The Phantom 'Rickshaw and other Eerie Tales (1888)
Wee Willie Winkie and Other Child Stories (1888)
Life's Handicap (1891)
The Light that Failed (1891) (novel)
American Notes (1891) (non-fiction)
The Naulahka: A Story of West and East (1892) (with Wolcott Balestie)
Many Inventions (1893)
The Jungle Book (1894)
Mowgli's Brothers (short story)
Kaa's Hunting (short story)
Tiger! Tiger! (short story)
The White Seal (short story)
Rikki-Tikki-Tavi (short story)
Toomai of the Elephants (short story)
Her Majesty's Servants (originally titled Servants of the Queen) (short story)
The Second Jungle Book (1895)
How Fear Came (short story)
The Miracle of Purun Bhagat (short story)
Letting in the Jungle (short story)
The Undertakers (short story)
The King's Ankus (short story)
Quiquern (short story)
Red Dog" (short story)
The Spring Running (short story)
Captains Courageous (1896) (novel)
The Day's Work (1898)
A Fleet in Being (1898)
Stalky & Co. (1899)
From Sea to Sea and Other Sketches, Letters of Travel (1899) (non-fiction)
Kim (1901) (novel)
Just So Stories for Little Children (1902)
Traffics and Discoveries (1904) (24 collected short stories)
With the Night Mail (1905) A Story of 2000 A.D
Puck of Pook's Hill (1906)

The Brushwood Boy (1907)
Actions and Reactions (1909)
A Song of the English (1909) (with W. Heath Robinson illustrator)
Rewards and Fairies (1910)
A History of England (1911) (non-fiction with Charles Robert Leslie Fletcher)
Songs from Books (1912)
As Easy as A.B.C. (1912) (Science-fiction short story)
The Fringes of the Fleet (1915) (non-fiction)
Sea Warfare (1916) (non-fiction)
A Diversity of Creatures (1917)
Land and Sea Tales for Scouts and Guides (1923)
The Irish Guards in the Great War (1923) (non-fiction)
Debits and Credits (1926)
A Book of Words (1928) (non-fiction)
Thy Servant a Dog (1930)
Limits and Renewals (1932)
Tales of India: the Windermere Series (1935)
Something of Myself (1937) (autobiography)
The Elephant's Child (fiction)

Autobiographies and Speeches
A Book of Words (1928)
Something of Myself (1937)

Short Story Collections
Quartette (1885) – with his father, mother, and sister
Plain Tales from the Hills (1888)
Soldiers Three, The Story of the Gadsbys, In Black and White (1888)
The Phantom 'Rickshaw and other Eerie Tales (1888)
Under the Deodars (1888)
Wee Willie Winkie and Other Child Stories (1888)
Life's Handicap (1891)
Many Inventions (1893)
The Jungle Book (1894)
The Second Jungle Book (1895)
The Day's Work (1898)
Life's Handicap (1899)
Stalky & Co. (1899)
Just So Stories (1902)
Traffics and Discoveries (1904)
Puck of Pook's Hill (1906)
Actions and Reactions (1909)
Abaft the Funnel (1909)
Rewards and Fairies (1910)
The Eyes of Asia (1917)
A Diversity of Creatures (1917)

Land and Sea Tales for Scouts and Guides (1923)
Debits and Credits (1926)
Thy Servant a Dog (1930)
Limits and Renewals (1932)

Military Collections

A Fleet in Being (1898)
France at War (1915)
The New Army in Training (1915)
Sea Warfare (1916)
The War in the Mountains (1917)
The Graves of the Fallen (1919)
The Irish Guards in the Great War (1923)

Poetry Collections

Schoolboy Lyrics (1881)
Echoes (1884) – with his sister, Alice ('Trix')
Departmental Ditties (1886)
Barrack-Room Ballads (1890)
The Seven Seas (1896)
An Almanac of Twelve Sports (1898, with illustrations by William Nicholson)
The Five Nations (1903)
Collected Verse (1907)
Songs from Books (1912)
The Years Between (1919)
Rudyard Kipling's Verse: Definitive Edition (1940)
The Muse Among the Motors (poetry)

Travel Writing

From Sea to Sea – Letters of Travel: 1887–1889 (1899)
Letters of Travel: 1892–1913 (1920)
Souvenirs of France (1933)
Brazilian Sketches: 1927 (1940)

Collected Works

The Outward Bound Edition (1897–1937, 36 volumes)
The Edition de Luxe (1897–1937, 38 volumes)
The Bombay Edition (1913–38, 31 volumes)
The Sussex Edition (1937–39, 35 volumes)
The Burwash Edition (1941, 28 volumes)

Poems

Departmental Ditties and Other Verses (1886)

Barrack Room Ballads (1889, republished with additions at later times)
The Seven Seas and Further Barrack-Room Ballads (In various editions 1891–96)
The Five Nations (with some new and some reprinted and revised poems, 1903)
Twenty-two original 'Historical Poems' (1911)
Songs from Books (1912)
The Years Between (1919)

Posthumous Collections
Rudyard Kipling's Verse: Definitive edition
A Choice of Kipling's Verse, edited by T.S. Eliot

In addition Kipling wrote and published many hundreds of poems too numerous to include here.